You Were There

A Rayburn High Romance
Book One

Melissa Knight

Cover Design by Jeanne Hancock

Dedicated to the students at Florida Parishes Juvenile Detention Center.

You are seen, and your voices are heard. You are loved.

Trust GOD from the bottom of your heart;
don't try to figure out everything on your own.
Listen for GOD's voice in everything you do, everywhere you go;
he's the one who will keep you on track.

Proverbs 3:5-6, The Message

PROLOGUE

It's not the end of the world.

Mother's words echoed in the sixteen-year-old girl's mind. From skinned knees to mean girl snubs, those words were a decent philosophy, a way to put things into perspective. She wasn't going to die. The sky would not fall.

Then again, her mother didn't know about *this* yet.

Fluffing her dark auburn hair, she studied herself in the mirror and reapplied lip gloss, steadying both her hand and her nerves. *Josh will know what to do. He loves me. We'll figure this out, and then we'll tell Mother together. S*he couldn't help a small shudder at that last thought, but she made herself stand tall, flipped her long hair over one shoulder and grabbed her purse and car keys. Josh only lived ten minutes away, but the day was too hot for walking.

Turning onto the street where Josh lived a few minutes later, she frowned. A couple of unfamiliar cars were parked in front of his house and another in the driveway. She pulled over in front of another house a couple of doors down, letting the car idle so the air conditioner would keep blowing. *Think.* Obviously, she should have called first. Josh's mother was uppity and would not like his girlfriend just showing up unannounced, especially if they had company.

Josh's mother. Shuddering again, she decided to leave and come back later.

But wait! There was Josh, tall and handsome with his blond hair and athlete's build, coming out of his front door, a huge grin on his face. Hot on his heels was a pretty, teenage girl with curly brown hair, wearing a halter top and short shorts. Hootchie-mama shorts, Mother would say with a sniff.

But Josh seemed to like them. Turning abruptly to face the brown-haired girl, he caught her in his arms, picking her up and twirling her around a time or two. Then he pressed her body, and her lips, close to his. They took their time in a leisurely kiss, unconcerned about being observed by anyone walking down the street or sitting alone in a nearby car.

When their lip lock ended, Josh and the smiling girl strolled casually, arm in arm, to one of the cars parked by the curb. Climbing into the passenger seat, Josh did not look around, never noticing the car idling down the street nor the girl behind its wheel.

That girl sat frozen, watching the scene in front of her unfold. She stared as the other girl drove away, carrying the boy she loved. She did not move and could barely think. She sat in that car for a long, long time.

The world did not end that day, she would remind herself later, much later. It just stopped with a shattering jolt, and then it started turning again, in a different direction.

As hard as that was, with familiar routines changing and private dreams drifting farther and farther away, she would never regret the single most important decision she had to make, in the days that followed.

The one that she made alone.

CHAPTER 1

"W-would you like to dance?" my date asked, barely meeting my eyes.

I smiled at Max, wanting to put him at ease. He was so nice. Careful. Respectful. I wondered if he could really dance, though.

"Let's show them how it's done!" I gestured toward the dance floor.

Taking a deep breath, Max followed me, plodding along like he was headed to his own execution, into the mass of teenagers currently busting moves and singing along with a top forty tune. I hummed it myself, nodding to the beat, and reached back to pull Max forward. He took my hand and squeezed it, sending a tiny alarm to my brain. *Whoa there, buddy.*

Waving at friends who were calling out and giving Max and me curious looks, I found some space and turned around to face him. I released his hand and he frowned, but I gave him my most charming smile. "We're going to have *fun*!" He recognized the words as a command, not an encouragement, because he gulped and bobbed his head.

"Start like this," I advised, and began a simple back and

forth step that he mastered within minutes. "Very good. Smile. When you smile, people think you're having a fun time even when you're not, and then after a while you discover you're enjoying yourself." *Sometimes,* I added silently, but I kept my voice perky. "Now, let's add some sass."

Taking his hand again, I lifted his arm and twirled underneath it. "Your turn," I sang out, and he attempted his own twirl. Somebody next to us called over "Look at Max go!" and though he turned beet red, he started loosening up.

The DJ chose a slow song next, and Max gave me a hopeful look, but I had my limits. "I'm parched," I announced, already starting to work my way back through the crowd. "Let's get a drink and find someplace to sit." Scanning the tables at the edges of the dance floor, I looked for any friend who was sitting this one out.

Sitting at a table later with Max, Abby, and a few other friends, I studiously avoided the gaze of someone else I had noticed here at Prom. He made a beeline for me anyway, dragging some poor girl behind him right off the dance floor.

"Reese," he growled, and I smiled at him.

"Ethan! Nice to see you! You know Max, don't you? And *you're* on the cheer squad, right?" I addressed this to his date, who was giving me a suspicious look.

"I made the squad for next year," the girl said, preening a bit. "I'm only a freshman."

"That's fantastic," I told her with sincerity. And then I closed my mouth, settled back in my chair, and waited.

Nobody else seemed to know what to say after that, and after much fidgeting and uncomfortable glances, Ethan and the girl drifted away. *Thank you, Grandma.* My grandmother wrote the book on social skills of all kinds, trust me, including how to disengage politely in delicate situations. A good thing, considering our family business.

"He's your ex-boyfriend?" Max tilted his head.

"He was never her boyfriend," Abby chimed in, leaning forward and grinning at me. "They hung out together, but that was all." I nodded at her, putting on my "what's a girl to do?" expression. Ethan had wanted more, and looking back, the fault was all mine. Guys seemed to think they had a claim on you if you spent time with them, and I should have known better.

Another fast song started, and I stood up. "Let's dance," I told Max, and he got up from his chair at once, appearing more cheerful this time.

"I'm ready to learn some more moves. You're a good teacher, Reese!" He hesitated. "Thanks." His eyes met mine, and I knew then that the two of us would be okay. Friends, nothing more.

I could always use another friend.

In my bedroom later, after Max had taken me home and we shook hands goodbye, laughing, my phone dinged with a text.

I finished removing my makeup and spent extra time brushing my hair and putting on my pajamas. There was only one text I wanted to see, and if this one was from someone else at least I could put off that feeling of disappointment for a while and keep the anticipation going.

Finally, I allowed myself to pick up the phone.

You home yet?

Sighing a little, I threw back the covers on my bed and burrowed underneath them, making myself cozy.

Yep. It was fun! Max is a nice guy. He'll be a good friend, I can tell.

There were lots of ways that Daniel could respond to this. He could say, "well, he'd better not be anything more than a friend!" or "I wish I had been your date" or even "how about a real date tomorrow night?"

The little line of dots bounced on my phone as Daniel typed a response.

I'm glad for you, Reese.

Turning onto my stomach, I analyzed his words and decided I liked them. They were undemanding. Supportive. He was happy for *me*. And for some reason, the way he usually included my name in a sentence felt intimate, as if he enjoyed the sound of it.

Before I could think of any response, his next words showed up.

Sweet dreams, gnite.

That was it?

I had to admit I felt disappointed. I wanted to tell him about teaching Max to dance, laugh about Ethan being all grouchy, analyze why junior prom was fun but just okay.

About how I wished I had been there with him, and not Max.

And that's when I reminded myself, sternly, that it was time to renew my vow.

High time.

Chapter 2

So, about that vow. It was simple.

I will not have another boyfriend in high school.

Period.

There were different ways this could be stated. I wouldn't agree to become anyone's girlfriend. I would not get serious about a guy. No male would make it beyond the friend zone. No matter how it was put, this was my decree. I could make a presentation with bullet points to support my reasons!

The bottom line was, I would never again allow some cute heartbreaker to make promises he could not, or would not, keep. My heart would never again be crushed, at least not in high school.

After that, I was a realist. There would be a thousand other things to think about after graduation, though, namely building my big, bright future starting with a business degree. That could certainly be done alone. I could only hope I would be a better judge of guys by then.

My best friend Casey, the only one who knew about my vow, remained unconvinced. I had discussed this with her after the awkward finish with Ethan.

"What about homecoming, and prom, and special events like that?" she had asked, her tone skeptical. "I know you can go alone, but you *enjoy* having dates, Reese! Guys are always asking you out, and most of them are sweet. You never know..." she paused and got that dreamy look, which meant she was thinking about her boyfriend Ben, the guy she was crazy about. He was certainly smitten with *her*. They were a goal couple.

I sighed. "Being invited to attend one dance and having a boyfriend are two different things. I'll be perfectly clear right from the start. Companionship and conversation only, no kissing. Maybe a little hug now and then, like friends do. As for the 'you never know' part, I *do* know. You struck gold with Ben, while I've just had one disaster after another."

Casey gave me a long look. "You kissed Daniel."

"On the cheek! That's allowed. It meant nothing." I was lying about the "nothing" part, and Casey knew it, but she didn't call me on it.

Daniel Dixon, Rayburn High's basketball star and A-plus potential valedictorian, chock full of swagger, had started paying attention to me this year in a bumbling way. For a guy who could probably date any girl he wanted, he didn't seem to know that, and he made this cute bargain with Casey to get "Reese advice" so I would go with him to Prom. She helped him out, but by the time he finally asked me it was too late. I had already accepted Max's invitation, so I had to turn Daniel down and I felt bad about it. That was all. It was an "I'm sorry" peck, not an "I'm devastated and in love with you" smooch.

After that kiss, though, standing in the hallway outside of our history classroom, Daniel looked at me, surprised, with those intense blue eyes. So gently, he reached over and tucked a stray lock of hair behind my ear and smiled. A yearning repeatedly buried over the years had reached up, eager for some long-denied sunshine radiating from that smile. Maybe he noticed that ache reflected in my eyes, because his own expression shifted, and his smile disappeared.

We could not get back into that classroom fast enough, and neither Daniel nor I had tried to recreate that tender moment. We still chatted and texted as friends do, and he surprised me with special snacks that he knew I liked now and then, but neither one of us brought up The Kiss again.

I wondered why he had been in so much of a hurry to get back into the classroom, though. Had my expression gone all crazy-needy, making him nervous and wanting to run the other way? Did he have his own vow, or plans which I didn't fit into?

If so, that was a good thing. I understood.

That rogue longing got stuffed right back into the Fantasyland section of my heart, where it belonged. As mentioned before, I had reasons. My history, and my mom's, and my grandmother's, spoke volumes. I didn't trust guys, and more importantly, I didn't trust my own judgment.

I would keep that vow. Friendzone only.

The next Monday morning I spotted the familiar little white bakery box on my desk when I walked into AP History. Daniel was already sitting at the desk behind mine, leaning back, his long legs sprawled underneath.

I groaned as I slid my backpack off my shoulder. "I'm gonna gain weight, Dixon!"

"Then I'll take it back," he retorted, and leaned forward, stretching his arm out to grab the box. I snatched it away before he could reach it, though, and read the label.

"Mmm, peanut butter chocolate! This one's a keeper.

Thank you." *You're a keeper too.* That thought got quickly squelched, and I sat down and focused on Casey, who sat one aisle over. She was watching me with great interest.

I raised my eyebrows at her, and she raised hers right back at me with this smirk on her face. Turning away, I started getting things out of my backpack.

Behind me, Daniel whispered, "You're welcome." The bell rang just then but I turned sideways anyway to give him a smile and assess the expression on his face. Or the *lack* of expression.

Because, you know what he did almost every time our eyes met lately? He shut down any emotion, his face a smooth mask of neutrality. At times I would catch a glimmer of something besides the usual confidence he exuded, but it always disappeared, making me think I imagined it.

The one and only time Daniel's eyes had held mine like a magnet, both of us unable to look away, was when I had given him that kiss on the cheek outside our history class. *That* was the expression I wished I could see again. His look had been warm and vulnerable, so unlike the cocky, sometimes arrogant guy I had known for years. It was as if we had truly seen each other for the first time.

This morning, I scanned Daniel's eyes as usual. I gave him nothing, and his own gaze remained bland. Turning back around, I straightened my shoulders and focused on our teacher. Mr. Langham was already starting to discuss our review schedule for the upcoming AP exam.

Far from shy, this boy was always giving me my favorite little treats and texting me sweet dreams, but he still shut me out. On the one hand, it didn't make sense, yet on the other, I understood completely.

Everyone has their back stories.

Chapter 3

"I just booked a fairy tale last night," Mom commented, typing on her laptop. "A Just Precious couple, straight up. Valentines Day."

"Hopefully, next February the fourteenth occurs on a weekend," Grandma said in her usual calm, measured voice, putting a plate of crisp waffles, browned to perfection, on the kitchen table. "I thought we already had a booking on that day."

"We have a morning vow renewal, but the fairy tale is booked in the evening. And yes, the fourteenth is on a Saturday next year."

I settled into my chair and reached for the blueberry syrup. When it came to Sunday morning brunches, my grandmother always put on a feast. Unless, of course, we had an event scheduled that morning.

You see, Grandma has a wedding planner business. She coordinates other events too, such as fancy baby showers, reunions, and company parties, but weddings are her bread and butter. Or more precisely, our waffles and syrup.

"I'm picturing a Cinderella," Mom said thoughtfully, still studying her screen.

"Always a favorite," Grandma agreed. "Leave that and come eat, Ruby. You're as thin as a rail. You too, Reese."

Mom pushed her laptop to the side of the table and grinned at me. Grandma was always telling us we were too thin, though we were both at healthy weights. We had quit correcting her long ago, and dutifully ate our waffles, spinach omelets, or whatever Grandma dished up each week.

"So, this couple is easy?" Grandma asked, settling down into her own chair.

"So far. But-"

"*It's early days yet!*" Grandma and I finished Mom's sentence with her.

By "couple," Grandma did not mean the bride and groom who were planning to get married. Oh, no. She meant the future bride and her *mother*. They were the ones usually making the big decisions about the ceremony and reception, and therefore the ones Grandma dealt with the most. Besides the bride, sometimes the groom was more involved, his own mother, or a random aunt, but usually the MOB- Mother Of the Bride- was the playmaker.

Let me explain some other terms Grandma had come up with, over the years at Your Perfect Day. This was the name of the business she started, ironically, after the worst day of her own life. More about that later.

A "Just Precious" couple (again meaning the bride and MOB, not the groom) were a pleasure to work with. Sane.

An "Oh, Honey" couple were needy, changing their minds frequently or requiring constant attention.

A "Bless Their Hearts" couple, on the other hand... well, that's a very diplomatic term for On the Edge of Insane. These were the Bridezilla folks, the complainers who were rude or acted entitled.

"Fairy Tale" meant a fairy tale wedding, usually involving a carriage ride for the couple, candles, and lots of golden touches. Other wedding themes Grandma had coordinated with exquisite attention to detail included garden, glamor, rustic and vintage. Rosalie Owens and Your Perfect Day were well known and respected in this town, and her business was expanding.

It had become *our* business in the last few years, in fact. Mom now worked full-time for Grandma, learning and taking over increased responsibilities. This summer, the one before my senior year, it was my turn. I would be an officially paid intern, learning the business from top to bottom.

Or more accurately, from bottom to top.

It was exciting, but I still shuddered as I used my knife to cut another piece of waffle. I would not allow those "bottom" jobs to put wrinkles on this seventeen-year-old face!

As if that first wrinkle had heard my thoughts, it started trying to form the very next Saturday.

I had helped at a few events before in minor ways, and this was a Just Precious couple's standard church wedding, so I wasn't expecting much drama. My role today was simply to shadow Mom, who was making sure everything was on point for the reception immediately following, at the country club.

Pulling up to the club near the service entrance, I turned into the parking space beside Mom's car. The florist's van was nearby, and I waved at Peter, the delivery guy who almost always set up the floral arrangements on weekends. He nodded at me, then shut the door of the van. "Well, I'm done here, and it sounds like you are too," he called over.

"Excuse me?" I asked him, smoothing the skirt of my light green dress as I got out of the car. "Why?"

He glanced towards the service entrance door, where Mom was just now hurrying out. "She'll explain. Gotta run, busy day. Good luck!" he said with exaggerated sympathy and went to get in his van.

I sighed before Mom even reached me. "Let me guess- the wedding has been called off? Are all the toilets overflowing in the club? Is cat hair in the cake?"

Mom laughed, which I took as a good sign. "Nothing like that, but you're needed at the church, pronto. One of the bridesmaids started throwing up and has a fever, and you're her replacement. Her dress should fit you." She looked quickly at my shoes. "You're already wearing nude heels, what a relief! Get going, honey. The ceremony is in less than an hour, and you'll have to do your own hair and makeup."

I gaped at her. "Seriously? The bridesmaid needs to be replaced? What difference-"

"Just go," Mom cut me off with a shrug. "The Just Precious couple is trending into Oh, Honey territory, according to Mother. The bride is freaking out because she thinks things will look off if there's not the same number of bridesmaids and groomsmen." She opened my car door and pointed inside. "Hurry."

"So, she's okay with having a complete stranger in her wedding?" I almost laughed, but I got back in the car, shaking my head.

At the church, I found the prep room where the bride and her attendants were getting ready. Harp music was already playing in the sanctuary, and I knew there was only about thirty minutes left before go time, walking down that aisle. Opening the door, I could literally hear all the women inside heave a sigh of relief.

Grandma came instantly to my side, holding a light pink gown. "Saved by the belle," she said, as calm as ever, but I saw a hint of exasperation on her face. "Here's the dress, Reese. Go change and Wendy here will fix your hair. You do your own makeup and lay it on thick for the pictures. You have fifteen minutes, tops."

I grimaced but she ignored me, turning around with a fixed smile to check on the bride. One of the bridesmaids touched my arm, shaking her head with a long-suffering look. "I'm Wendy, hon." She lowered her voice to a whisper. "There was vomit, and the bride was having a hissy fit, and then you come in to save the day! We've got your back." She closed her eyes in what appeared to be a silent prayer, then opened them to assess me. "That beautiful auburn hair won't take much fixin.' And you're as pretty as a picture, with those hazel eyes! You don't even need makeup. But do it for the *pictures*." The way she said it made me giggle, and with her help, in fourteen minutes flat I was deemed presentable.

"Just copy the others," Grandma instructed a bit later, when it was my turn to walk down the church aisle. "You'll do fine."

And I did. The only thing I struggled with was trying to keep a straight face when I glanced at the groomsman who was obviously paired with me, standing on the groom's side at the front of the church. He was studying me looking puzzled but gave me this little wink anyway.

Then, as I walked back down the aisle on his arm after the ceremony was over, I saw another face watching me in surprise, but this one was familiar. I grinned at him and gave him my own little wink.

Daniel.

CHAPTER 4

He found me later at the reception. I was standing next to Mom in a relatively calm moment, surveying the dance floor. She and I had been busy making sure everything was flowing smoothly, from overseeing the cake cutting to checking in with the caterers and deejay, on alert for any potential issues. I had long since changed back into my own green dress, once the formal wedding pictures were done. As for Daniel- oh *my*.

Casually debonaire in his dark suit and tie, his light brown hair just a tad unruly, this was a different look from his usual hoodie and track pants at school. I liked it. I liked it a lot.

Clearing his throat, Daniel greeted Mom politely, then turned to me. "I have questions."

"And I have answers," I told him, grinning. "But I'm sort of working right now. Have you met my mom?" I introduced the two of them, knowing full well that Mom's daughter radar was now on full alert.

"Nice to meet you, Daniel. And Reese, you just go take a nice long break and answer this young man's questions, okay? I'll text you if I need your help."

I was only too glad to take her up on that offer. "Sounds great! I would love to take off my heels and sit down right now."

"So, you're a friend of my cousin?" Daniel asked, as he led me to the most distant table from the dance floor. There was an older couple sitting on one side watching the dancing, but Daniel pulled a chair out for me at the other end.

Grandma would approve. The boy had manners! I also appreciated the fact that his soap, or aftershave, or whatever it was that he was wearing, smelled very, very attractive.

I sank into the chair, immediately kicking off my heels, and Daniel sat down beside me. I got another whiff of that minty, clean smell. "If you mean the bride, I actually don't even know her," I admitted. "We just met tonight when one of the bridesmaids got sick. My grandmother is your cousin's wedding planner." I gave him a brief rundown of the situation, and the whole time Daniel listened attentively, chuckling in all the right places.

"That sounds like my cousin. She's chill until something goes wrong, and then she overreacts. Her new husband will have his hands full." He grinned, looking directly into my eyes, and my heart skipped a beat.

Steeling myself, I looked away quickly. "Is there a water bottle in this place?"

"Well, you should know, right? Since you're one of the planners?" Daniel reached over and squeezed my arm gently, then stood up. "You stay put and I'll find you one. Be right back!"

I stared at my arm where Daniel had touched it, feeling downright breathless. Once he returned, the practical, resolute Reese was telling me I should grab the water bottle and run. Find Mom. Create a problem to take care of, if necessary, just to keep myself busy.

Another Reese was telling me to stay, to enjoy Daniel's

easygoing company and relax. This was the Reese I didn't trust, though. The one with poor judgment. The one I tried to keep from making important decisions.

Looking out over the country club ballroom, I followed Daniel's tall figure making his way to the refreshments area and watched him until he came back to the table, carrying two water bottles.

Making myself stand up, I gave him an apologetic look. "Thanks, Daniel. I need to get back now, sorry."

He didn't even blink and handed me a bottle. "I understand. I should probably be sociable and go talk to my family members. You know how it is."

I clutched the cold bottle. "I do know how it is. You take care." I started to brush past him, and he spoke one more time.

"Hey, Reese?" His voice was low, and I hesitated, glancing up at him. I was glad I did, because before he could get that mask of emotional invisibility on completely, his eyes gave a couple of those emotions away.

The warmth and interest were unmistakable. "Yes?" My voice was just above a whisper.

"I..." Daniel swallowed and the mask clicked into place. It seemed to take more effort this time, however. "You look beautiful tonight. I'm glad I got to see you."

With everything that was within me, I wanted to kiss that boy again. On the cheek, of course.

Instead, bending to pick up my almost-forgotten heels, but not taking the time to put them back on, I fled.

"So, Daniel seems like a polite young man. And so handsome," Mom said the next morning as soon as I appeared in the kitchen, still in my pajamas. Seated at the table, she was already holding a cup of coffee, and Grandma stood by the sink.

"Daniel? Who is this? Have I met him?" Grandma looked from Mom to me. "What did I miss?"

"Well, good morning to ya'll too," I drawled, surveying the table where Sunday brunch was laid out, complete with a riotous bunch of spring flowers in a crystal vase. Hmm, it was quiche and bacon today, one of my favorite combos. "May I please just get some juice and take one little bite of food before the interrogation begins? Not that there's any big reveal."

"Take *two* bites!" Grandma replied. "More coffee, Ruby?"

"Yes, please," Mom said, covering a yawn. "Although I should be serving *you*, Mother. Spoiling us like this every Sunday! You know I can take my turn cookin'."

"Pshaw!" Grandma said briskly, but she looked pleased as she poured more coffee into Mom's cup. "You both need a little spoiling occasionally. And I want us to make our own special memories at least one morning a week, and not just create them for others the rest of the time! Now, who is this Daniel?"

Yep, by then I had taken exactly two bites.

"Daniel Dixon is a friend from school. We've known each other for years. He was at the wedding last night because the bride is his cousin, and we talked at the reception for a few minutes. That's it. No more."

There was more, of course, but nothing they needed to know. They didn't need to know that Daniel had asked me to prom, or that he brought me little treats now and then, or that he had made the effort to get to know me better lately. They absolutely did not need to know that I had kissed him on the cheek.

And heaven forbid they found out that I had wanted to kiss him again last night.

My words seemed to satisfy them, and we all sat quietly for a few minutes eating our food, or so I assumed.

"A penny for your thoughts, Ruby," Grandma commented,

and I glanced over at Mom. She was holding her fork, resting it on her plate, but was staring into space. Her food, and her full cup of coffee, looked untouched.

"Mom?" I questioned when she didn't respond to Grandma's words after several seconds.

Her gaze turned to me. "You said Daniel's last name is Dixon?"

I studied her face. "Yes? Do you know any Dixons?"

Mom glanced at Grandma, who seemed only mildly interested in her answer, and then exhaled a breath I didn't know she had been holding. "Honey, we work with so many families in this business. I'm sure that name has come up. Hey, we have a free afternoon! So how are we going to spend it?"

Grandma and I looked at each other, both noticing her change of subject.

"Free for you," I reminded them, reaching for another piece of bacon. "Not for me. Finals are just around the corner, you know. Projects are coming due, there are teachers to please, essays to write, corporations to take over, worlds to conquer, that sort of thing."

"Bodies to bury," Mom added, not blinking an eye.

"That's my girl," Grandma said proudly, and I squinted at her, chewing my bacon. I honestly didn't know if she was referring to my plans or to her own daughter's comment.

CHAPTER 5

Maybe Mom was serious about having bodies to bury, because covering up a murder seemed like a big enough sin to get her to make her announcement to me, later that evening. I was sitting at my desk finishing up homework, but her words made me stop and turn around, math now completely forgotten.

"You're going to church with me on Wednesday night?" I repeated, puzzled. "It's a youth group, Mom, not for adults."

Mom shook her head, leaning against my open door. "I didn't mean I was going with you and Casey to that youth meeting. Karen has been inviting me to her Bible study for a long time now, and I've decided to give it a whirl."

Karen was Casey's mother, and she and Mom had hit it off when they met almost a year ago. Her whole family went to church regularly and I went with Casey to her youth group meetings, off and on. I supposed this Wednesday would be one of the "on" nights.

"I'm guessing the Bible study meets at the same time? I thought you said church is full of hypocrites."

"Yes, it's at the same time, and yes, I have made that statement, but Karen doesn't seem that way. And you enjoy that youth group. So, I'm going to check out the Bible study and give it a fair shake."

I considered this. I did like Casey's youth group. Several of my friends went to the meetings, even those who didn't go to church any other time, and I felt welcomed and comfortable there. For me it was a social thing, a way to hang out with a group I was learning to trust. I think those same friends would be shocked to know my private opinion about God, though.

Namely, did such a being even exist?

Never one to mince words, another trait of the Owens women, I asked Mom the obvious.

"Do you believe in God?"

Mom closed her eyes and crossed her arms almost defensively, still leaning against the door. "I should be a better mother to you, Reesie," she replied, her eyes still shut. "I should tell you yes, that I have no doubts. I should have taken you to Sunday School when you were a little girl-"

"Mom! Stop!" I told her, a little annoyed but also amused. "Just answer the question without all the drama!"

Mom opened her eyes and sighed, giving me a lopsided grin. Uncrossing her arms, she walked over to my chair and wrapped them around my neck in a loose hug.

"I love you, Reese. And because of you, honestly, I'm going to give God a chance. I do believe he's out there somewhere. I just don't know where. Not in my life, it seems."

We were quiet for a moment, her arms still around me.

"Why do you think he's out there?" I asked seriously. I needed to know this.

"Because he gave me you," she whispered. "Only God could have given me a daughter like you. Only someone who knows me and loves me an awful lot."

And with that she let me go, giving me a wink, and left the

room. My eyes filled with tears, and not because her words had been so sweet.

Those tears were there because instead of seeing sadness in her eyes, the heaviness I caught glimpses of over the years, I had seen hope. Lightness.

And her hope, in turn, made my own heart feel a little lighter.

Later that night, lying in bed, I texted Casey.

> My mom is going with your mom to that Bible study on Wednesday night.

Casey's response was immediate.

> Cool! Your mom is the best. And you're her little mini!

I smiled. I *did* look exactly like Mom, and people often mistook her for my older sister. We were alike in so many ways, which was part of the reason I had made my vow. I did not want to repeat her mistakes.

Mom had become a mother at seventeen. After becoming pregnant the summer before her senior year, she went to live with her older sister, my Aunt Rachel, who was married with kids and living in Atlanta. When I was five years old, she moved us back here to her hometown, equipped with her GED and a hard-won cosmetology license. Mom built a loyal clientele in a hair salon while working for Your Perfect Day on weekends. Grandma helped us when she could, but it was mainly just the two of us, me and Mom.

Well, *mostly* just the two of us. With her dark auburn hair (just like mine), perfect complexion and sparkling hazel eyes, Mom was a guy magnet, and still so young. Unfortunately, not all guys are a dream come true once you get past their good-lookin' exteriors, and Mom must have gotten burned a lot. She had gone through several boyfriends by the time I was fifteen. To be fair, in whatever way those guys failed my mother, they were all kind to me. Decent people.

When I was fifteen, however, we moved in with Grandma, to the house where Mom had grown up. Grandma was overjoyed, though I knew Mom was reluctant. For her it must have seemed like a sign of weakness, a sacrifice of independence. I think she felt embarrassed about it, but I knew she had made the move for me.

At only fifteen I had made a couple of poor decisions myself, trusting guys who said they loved me, and I was hurting. Mom found out and resolved to put us in what she felt was a more "stable environment," whatever that meant. Whether it was the right decision or not, the move back to her childhood home was for *me*.

Make no mistake, I adored Grandma's stately house, exquisitely decorated and elegant on both the inside and out. My beautiful pale blue bedroom, with white oak furniture and gauzy curtains at the windows, made this private refuge both pretty and comfortable. Not to mention I had my own bathroom! And for all of her sometimes overbearing ways, I loved Grandma.

Smiling, I rolled over on my side and looked at the other text, the one I hadn't answered yet.

> Is your brain fried from all this homework? Mine is!

Daniel. I typed my reply.

> I doubt that. You're so smart I bet your brain is thirsty for even more.

As soon as I hit "send," I regretted those words. Did they sound gushy, flattering his intellect like some swoony fangirl? That was not my intention, I was not that girl...

His response came seconds later.

> True. I'm reading Einstein's theory of relativity at this very moment.

I sighed, relieved.

> Go to bed, you goon. Gnite.

I rolled on my back, ready to nestle under the covers, but I didn't relax until I heard the quiet ping of his reply.

> Gnite Reese. Sleep well.

I did.

CHAPTER 6

"So, do ya'll want to meet this weekend and study together for the AP exam?" Casey looked at Daniel and me expectantly.

History class was over, and I had to rush across campus to get to my next class, but I nodded up and down. "Absolutely. The U.S. History exam is supposedly one of the hardest ones. I need all the quizzing I can get."

"Okay. Are you game, Dixon?"

"Oh, I suppose." He stretched out his arms lazily, then hitched his backpack onto his shoulder. "I usually float my kayak alone, but I'll have mercy on you ladies and help you out."

"Don't strain yourself," Casey retorted. "Although we could help you improve your humility skills on the side. Oh wait, you don't have any, I forget."

Daniel just grinned. He and Casey always went back and forth like this, though it was good-natured. They had to debate each other once in English last year, and their competitive streaks just seemed to flare up around each other. "So, Friday night?"

Casey met my eyes and we both shook our heads. "Nope,

we've already planned a sleepover study night," Casey informed him. "How about Saturday? Are you busy with a wedding that day, Reese?"

"There *is* a wedding that night, but I'm not helping. Mom insists I take the whole weekend for studying, so either Saturday or Sunday is fine with me. Text me later, though. I've gotta run!" I hustled towards the door, leaving Daniel and Casey to finalize the plan.

Later, sitting at a table outside during lunch, I checked my phone and saw a group text message including Daniel, me, Casey and her boyfriend, Ben.

Saturday, Daniel's house at 2 pm.

Hmmm, Daniel's house? It would be interesting to see where he lived and maybe meet his parents. I wondered if he had siblings, and what his room looked like, what he had on his walls...

Stop it, I told myself, squeezing my eyes shut.

"Stop what?" One of my friends, holding a sandwich halfway to her mouth, looked at me curiously. Had I really said those words out loud?

"Oh, I just- I was thinking about someone. Some*thing*." I corrected myself quickly and good heavens, I blushed.

She gave me a strange look, and no wonder. Reese Owens does not lose her composure. She does not stumble in her words, and she does not blush.

Giving a little shrug that hopefully looked careless, I took a long, long drink out of my water bottle.

When I arrived at Daniel's address on Saturday afternoon, I saw Ben's truck already parked by the curb, which meant Casey was there as well. Ben was also taking the AP exam next week, though he was in a different class. Parking my car behind his truck, I took a minute to study the outside of Daniel's home.

Smaller than Grandma's house, it was in an older neighborhood with plenty of shady, mature trees. A wide porch stretched across the entire front of the house, and white trim railings flanked the broad concrete steps leading up to the front door. Bright red geraniums in terra cotta pots lined the steps. The scene was cozy and charming, and I was interested to see how the home was decorated on the inside.

Daniel opened the front door before I even made it to the porch. "I see the basketball hoop!" I called out, motioning toward the driveway. "Is this where Rayburn High's mighty sports legend shot his first basket?"

"That is correct," Daniel responded with a straight face. "A commemorative plaque will soon be installed for my fans."

"I'm sure the two of them will appreciate that so much," I responded sweetly, and Daniel laughed, an appreciative gleam in his eyes. His delight was contagious, and I also started giggling, both of us now standing on the porch.

"Not you too, Reese," Daniel finally said, still chuckling. "Your friend Casey in there beats up my ego every chance she gets."

"I heard my name," a voice called from inside the house, and Casey came to the front door, looking expectantly from me to Daniel. "What's this about an ego? Talking about yourself again, Dixon?"

"See what I mean? I can't catch a break." Daniel and I grinned at each other.

Somebody cleared his throat, and it took me a second for the sound to register. Breaking my gaze from Daniel's, I turned to the door and saw that Ben was behind Casey, both watching us with great interest.

How long had Daniel and I been standing there, staring at each other?

"Let's get this study session started." My voice was brisk, every trace of humor gone.

"We're burning daylight," Daniel agreed, motioning for me to go into the house ahead of him. His voice sounded just as somber as mine. I did not allow myself another look at him, but I did glance at Casey, expecting to see that teasing look on her face. It wasn't there, though. Instead, she looked bemused.

The four of us powered through U.S. History for almost two and a half hours before Daniel's mother entered the living room. "Snacks, anyone?" she called out, and we all cheered.

"Yes, ma'am!" Ben answered for all of us. Mrs. Dixon beamed.

"I figured you would need a break. I've been trying to stay out of your way while you studied, but I'm getting hungry myself. Working outside in the garden does that to a person. Now, I've met Ben, but who are these two beautiful young ladies, Daniel?"

Daniel introduced Casey first, and Mrs. Dixon chuckled. "Oh, now I meet the famous Casey who debated my son last year! I hear you're very smart!" Casey raised her eyebrows at Daniel after she thanked Mrs. Dixon, and he shrugged.

"And you are Reese," she said softly to me. To my surprise she reached for my hand and held it gently, like I might want to break away. "I'm so pleased to finally meet you. Welcome to our home." Her blue eyes, so like Daniel's, radiated kindness.

"I love the front of your house," I told her. "And the way you've decorated inside. It's all very pretty and welcoming."

She dipped her chin, accepting my compliment. "You notice these things. I like that." She let go of my hand. "Now, let's all go into the kitchen and see what snacks we can find."

As we followed her towards the kitchen, I allowed myself a

peek at Daniel. I wondered what he had told his mother about me, since she said she was pleased to "finally" meet me.

As if our awareness of each other was connected by some invisible string, Daniel looked my way at the same time. He sidled up next to me briefly and I instinctively slowed down, lagging a step behind as the others went ahead of us into the kitchen.

"I told her you were special," he whispered, before he also disappeared into the kitchen. I was right on his heels, but I'm glad nobody paid any attention to me as I entered the tidy, sunshine-filled room. My heart was pounding after hearing those quiet words, and my mind went into overdrive with hope, fear, joy and dread all swirling together.

Even if this boy couldn't exactly read my mind, he seemed very much in tune with my thoughts. He was sensitive and kind, plus all those little details like being tall, smart, handsome, funny... and now he had a mama who liked me, and he told her I was special?

I was in so much trouble.

"You okay?" Casey asked me a little later, drawing me aside as the boys and Mrs. Dixon chatted over microwaved burritos, chips, and salsa.

"Yes," I responded automatically, then looked down at my still-empty paper plate, clutching it in both hands like a life preserver. Heaving a sigh, I gave up. "I mean, no. Daniel and I need to talk."

She nodded, took me by the arm, and led me to the array of food laid out on the kitchen counter. "Eat something," she told me firmly, then joined in the conversation going on about space travel, of all things. Trust me, if someone was selling a ride to Mars right now, I would have bought that ticket.

Distracted, it took me a minute to realize that the conversation had changed from space to sleepovers. In particular, the sleepover I hosted at my house last night.

"You actually *studied*?" Ben sounded skeptical, raising an eyebrow at Casey. "What was the subject? Who the best-looking guys are at Rayburn High? Or the dumbest?"

"I'm at the top of that first list, and I could make an educated guess about the second one," Daniel said with his usual confidence, and Casey rolled her eyes. Amused, I looked around to see Mrs. Dixon's reaction, but she had left the kitchen.

"We each chose what final to study for," Casey informed Ben. She launched into a brief outline of what we usually did at our sleepovers, leaving out any potentially embarrassing information, of course.

Daniel interrupted her in the middle of a sentence. "Whoaa, wait a sec," he said, holding out his hand like a stop sign. "You girls play truth or dare? Seriously? Isn't that a little, um-"

"Middle school?" Ben finished for him, and they both snickered. "No offense," he told Casey and me, obviously trying to keep a straight face.

"None taken," Casey told him haughtily. "Clearly, sharing innermost thoughts is not something that guys like to do."

"Amen to that," I seconded. "But it's not like we have to say anything we feel uncomfortable about. Our rule is to just tell the truth, or we can pass. We have *guidelines*. The goal is to..." I searched for the right words. "To get to know each other better, not to embarrass anyone. Our friendships have become closer."

"And we've had a lot of laughs." Casey and I grinned at each other. What an understatement!

An alarm on Ben's phone started beeping and he glanced at it, turning it off. "Hey, I hate to break this up, but you and I have to go," he told Casey, and she nodded in agreement.

"I do, too." No way would I stay here when they left, alone with Daniel. He had been quiet during my truth or dare explanation and was now watching me thoughtfully. "Let's, um, get the kitchen cleaned up first, though."

Between the four of us, it only took minutes to put food away and leave the kitchen spotless. I grabbed my backpack, preparing to leave as soon as Casey and Ben did so I could get out of this charming house, away from this guy who was taking up way too much space in my head, and find a quiet place to think. *Think.*

Daniel's question was unexpected, as I started to open the front door. "Reese, could we meet somewhere tomorrow and talk?"

My hand froze on the doorknob. Casey also stopped right behind me, going completely still. I didn't know if Ben was surprised or not, though I would bet a hundred dollars he was grinning.

I turned around slowly to face Daniel. "Yes?" My voice was a squeak, and Grandma's words came to mind. *Stiffen your spine, girl.* I immediately stood up straighter. "Yes," I repeated, my voice cool and steady. "Text me later."

"Well, let's go!" Casey said brightly, pushing me a bit, and I opened the door.

My spine might have stiffened up, but my thoughts?

They were like leaves blowing in a gust of wind.

CHAPTER 7

As I got ready for bed that night, Daniel had still not texted, but I did get a message from Casey.

> Have you been looking at any social media? Daniel wanted me to ask you. I don't know why. I just checked and don't see anything unusual.

Hmmm. I quickly scrolled through my social media accounts. I didn't see any reason for concern either, and I wasn't tagged on any posts.

> I don't see anything that interesting. Why wouldn't he just ask me directly?

Before she could respond, however, another text came from Mia.

> Did you see Ethan's post earlier?

Frowning now, I checked again, going directly to Ethan's

accounts this time. There was still nothing of interest, nothing recently posted.

I texted Mia.

> What did he post?

Her response was quick.

> He took it down, but you should know about this. I took a screen shot.

Sitting down on my bed, a feeling of dread settled over me. What on earth would Ethan put on social media that was so alarming? Something about me, obviously. Before I could speculate any further, the screenshot came through.

I looked at the image carefully. It was a picture of me at the Sadie Hawkins dance a couple of months ago, wearing that pale pink dress I loved. I was smiling and there was nothing unusual about the picture. It was the caption, however, that made me literally gasp out loud.

Horrible, lewd words, calling me a name you don't say in polite company.

Another text came from Mia.

> Don't let it get to you, Reese. I only sent it because you'll hear about it anyway and I want you to be prepared. Ethan's a jerk and everyone knows it. His words are garbage.

Garbage.

My first reaction was rage. Pacing around my room, I looked for something to throw, preferably at Ethan and preferably sharp. I should call him and give him a piece of my mind! Why would he do this to me? Was he seriously still hung up on me not being his prom date? I had never done anything wrong to him. We had been friends, nothing more than that, even though he wanted more.

I reached for my phone, which by now was buzzing with incoming texts. but then my hand stilled. *Had* I been at fault? Was I the kind of girl that deserved the label Ethan gave me, a girl who teased and led guys on? Sitting down on the bed again, I searched my memory for an indication of that girl, and I winced.

At fifteen I knew I had gone too far with a couple of boys. Each time, I thought I had loved them. They didn't force me to do anything, and I could only blame my own poor judgment. Though I hoped for it, the love I felt had not been the lasting kind, not what I pictured true love to really be. Obviously, I was young and immature, but hey, it was only two years ago. Could I really grow that much wiser in just two years? Doubtful.

I laid down on the bed, my knees curled up to my chest with my arms wrapped around them. About a year ago, I had a crush on Casey's older stepbrother, Jackson. He was a good guy, a Christian like Casey, and so sweet to me. I had thrown myself at him, wanting to date him so badly, and we had even gone to a dance together at my invitation. Jackson was a perfect gentleman and we had fun, but ultimately, he had chosen someone else. I didn't deserve him, and he must have recognized that. Though we were still friends, I wasn't good enough to be his girlfriend. I had accepted this at the time and allowed that sad thought to settle again into my heart. It had happened. It was true.

As for Ethan? It had been fun spending time with him, and he seemed nice. He even went to Casey's youth group at her church for a while, though he stopped coming after that Sadie Hawkins dance when I reminded him we were just friends.

Yes, he was self-centered and barely listened to me. He never asked about my opinions or tried to get to know me well, but we all have our faults, right? We hung out together because he gave me attention and was fun to be around, though looking back I had to admit it was a barely-skim-the-surface friendship. We never even held hands, yet I still shouldn't have been so naive. I *did* lead him on, even if I didn't mean to. I had hurt him. That made me a bad person, and he knew it. I knew it.

I did not cry. I laid in bed, wide awake, making lists of all the things I knew were wrong with me. All the reasons I could not trust my judgment, and certainly not any emotion. Ethan shouldn't have posted that picture and said those words about me, but I deserved it, nonetheless.

Reaching for my phone, I examined the screenshot again, feeling numb inside. I had missed calls from Mia, Casey, and a couple of other friends, but there was no word from Daniel. He had probably seen Ethan's post and decided to have nothing else to do with me, to put the brakes on even our friendship. I didn't deserve Daniel either, so I understood. He was too sweet, too smart, too kind. He deserved someone better than that girl in Ethan's post.

It was the last thought that broke me. My breathing hitched, and I knew the dam holding back my tears was about to break. Before it did, another text came through.

Daniel.

You awake? Can I call you?

I sent a text to Mom, telling her I didn't feel well and was going to sleep in late tomorrow morning.

Then I turned off the phone and cried myself to sleep.

CHAPTER 8

The knock at my door the next morning was soft but insistent. "Reese?" Mom's voice

I groaned, rolling over. Didn't she get my text message last night?

"Reese, I'm coming in." She opened my door, and I burrowed under the covers, hiding my face completely. Very mature, yes.

"Honey, what's wrong? You're not feeling well?"

"Not really," I croaked, not even having to fake my weak voice.

"Well, let me take your temperature. Mother and I have an afternoon baby shower at the country club, remember? But I'm not going to leave you here alone if you're sick."

"Aaaaaghhh." I had forgotten about that gig. I couldn't make Mom miss work when I wasn't really sick. Not physically, anyway.

"Besides that..." Mom paused. "Well, you have a friend downstairs who insists on seeing you."

Casey? Or Mia? It had to be one of them. I sighed and reluctantly pulled the covers down from my face. "I'm not sick,

Mom, I'm just super tired." Which was true. I hadn't slept well, and I was sick and tired of myself.

Mom came over and sat on the side of the bed, reaching over to touch my forehead. "You don't feel warm." She studied my face. "What's going on, baby girl?"

Her gentle voice made me tear up again and I swallowed. "Oh Mom, it's just...something I don't want to talk about right now. I will though, I promise I will. Just not now, okay? I'm all right. Go take care of the baby shower. I'll be fine."

I forced a smile which didn't fool Mom a bit, and she sighed. "I'll check with you right before we leave and make no mistake, I won't go unless I'm sure you're okay. Now, get up and get dressed for your visitor."

Yawning, I got out of bed and headed for the bathroom. "Just send Casey up here, Mom. Or Mia, whoever it is."

"Actually no, Reese, you'll have to get dressed and go downstairs." Mom's voice sounded faintly amused, and I paused to look at her before opening the bathroom door. "Your visitor is male, and boys are not allowed in your room. He's in the kitchen eating some of that brunch you missed."

I gaped at her.

"It's your friend, Daniel Dixon. And let's just say he doesn't look too good, either." She turned and walked to the door. "I'll tell him you'll be down in five minutes."

Looking at my reflection in the bathroom mirror a minute later, I knew there was no way I could hide the traces of my rough night in five- no, four- minutes. *But what does it matter?* My mind returned to the dreary conclusions from last night's events. *Let him see me at my worst.* With that thought came another -the image Ethan had posted. *Actually, he already has.*

I threw on an old Rayburn High t-shirt and shorts, pulled my hair back in a messy ponytail - not the cute kind of messy-

and trudged downstairs, trying to stiffen my spine with every step I took.

If Daniel was surprised by my unusually sloppy appearance he gave no indication. In all fairness, however, it would probably have been painful for him to change facial expressions, since that boy was sporting the ugliest, most bruised-up black eye I had ever seen.

I gasped.

"What on earth? Your poor eye!" I walked quickly over to the kitchen table where he was seated, a few pancake crumbs left on his almost-empty plate. "Daniel, what happened to you?"

He managed a grin, though it could have been a grimace. "You should see the other guy."

"What other guy? Who?" My mind started racing, though lack of sleep and the descent into my own big pit of depression last night wasn't good for the brain cells. I pulled out a chair across the table from Daniel and sank into it. He remained silent, though he wiped some syrup off his mouth with a napkin rather gingerly. That's when I noticed he also had a split lip. What?

"Those are the best pancakes I've ever had in my life," he confided. "Don't tell my mom that."

"Start explaining," I ordered him. "Now. Everything. Including why you are sitting here in my kitchen eating pancakes."

"Don't be rude, Reese," Grandma interjected, bustling into the kitchen wearing a simple yet elegant lavender dress. "I have enjoyed this young man's company this morning, since you did not join us for brunch yourself. Are you still feeling sick?"

I watched Daniel's eyes narrow at me- well, at least the one that wasn't blackened. "You're sick?"

"I'm fine, Grandma, just tired," I told her, scrutinizing Daniel right back. "You and Mom go manage that baby shower. Make it a perfect day for the new mom."

Grandma accepted this and addressed Daniel. "Now, you put more ice on that eye soon. Do you need anything else, dear? More bacon?"

"I'm not one to turn down bacon, ma'am," he said solemnly. "But I do believe I'm full. Thank you for this fine breakfast."

"Brunch," she corrected him, but she looked pleased and patted him on the shoulder. She turned to me next, studying my face. "You'll be fine," she said softly. You're strong, Reese."

And with that she walked out the door, leaving me still trying to process what was happening. Grandma often told me to be strong, but why did she reassure me of that right now? Only because she thought I was tired? Why did she seem to be buddies with Daniel?

Mom popped in the kitchen at that point. "Reese, if you're truly not sick, then Mother and I will leave in less than half an hour." She gave Daniel a pointed look. "I'm sorry, but you'll have to leave when we do."

"Oh of course, Mrs. Owens," Daniel replied hastily. "I'll just be another few minutes. I wanted to check on Reese since she's so ... tired."

Mom's face softened. "It's *Miss* Owens, but you can call me Miss Ruby. I need to gather up some things, but I'll be back in about twenty minutes." After another searching look at me, she left the room.

Daniel took Mom's timeline very seriously because he got right down to business. "You saw Ethan's post yesterday?"

I nodded. "Mia sent it to me. Explain the black eye."

He sighed ruefully and looked down at his plate. "Those were such great pancakes."

"DIXON!" I slammed my hand down on the table in frustration, and he smiled, sort of.

"After I saw that post last night, it made me mad, of course. So, I went right over to that moron's house to talk to him."

I raised one eyebrow. Obviously, a whole lot more than just talking had gone on.

"I rang the doorbell, and one of his football buddies answered. A few guys were there at his house hanging out, so I asked Ethan if I could talk to him alone." He sighed. "As it turns out, it wouldn't have mattered since they were all in on the joke, as they called it. Then again, they had been drinking.

"Anyway, Ethan and I went out on the front porch, I told him to take down that social media post, and he punched me. I never saw it coming. In fact, he got another good punch in before I could react. I'm not proud of that."

There was a gleam in his good eye, however. "Fortunately, my uncle is a cop, and he taught me a few self-defense moves. Therefore, Ethan's not looking too pretty, either. His buddies finally realized what was going on, and they came outside and broke things up. Good thing, too. That guy's got some muscle on him.

"But I have faster reflexes." He grinned cockily. "And I'm smarter."

I just sat there, stunned.

"So," he went on after a small pause, "about that time Ethan's parents got home and they figured out the situation fast. The post was taken down quickly, especially since I informed them he could face legal charges."

Daniel leaned across the table and held out his hand. Surprised, I stared at it, and he wiggled his fingers at me. "Take my hand," he asked softly, and I did, hesitantly. What was this?

He held on firmly, yet his touch was gentle. "You might be able to press charges, Reese. Cyberbullying is against the law. If you do, you have plenty of witnesses to support you. Evidence. Lots of friends. I would back you one hundred percent." He squeezed my hand, and his expression went fierce.

"Everything he said was a lie. Don't let his words get in your head, Reese, none of it. You're amazing." He swallowed. "You're... radiant. Intelligent. Beautiful inside and out."

After all the shame and guilt I had accepted the night before, his words were soothing, like putting a bandage over an open wound. But bandages only cover things up temporarily. The wound was still there.

I managed a smile, though. Holding his hand felt good, and not in just some romantic way. I soaked in his loyalty, his kindness, his strength.

Mom walked in the room at that exact moment, her gaze immediately zeroing in on our hand-holding scene. "Time's up, Daniel. It was nice seeing you again. Want an ice pack to go?"

"No, ma'am. I'm heading straight home, and we've got plenty of ice there. And pain meds." He released my hand and stood up.

Looking at Daniel in consternation, all the questions I should have asked started coming to mind one after another. He was in pain? What did his parents think about all of this? Did he get in trouble for getting into a fight, even though it was self-defense? Did Ethan have a black eye too?

I got up and walked Daniel to the front door, trying to assemble my thoughts. "Daniel, I still have questions. Could we talk later? Also, I never thanked you." I looked up at him, not even trying to disguise the admiration I knew was on my face. "You defended me. Took a hit for me, even."

He shrugged. "I'd do it again. I'll call you later, okay?"

I nodded and opened the front door, where yet another

surprise greeted me. There, parked behind Daniel's car, was a white truck. It was Ben's, full of passengers who came piling out when they saw me and Daniel at the door- Ben, Casey, Mia, and Abby.

Reinforcements had arrived, and just as holding Daniel's hand had reassured me, the look of concern on my friends' faces made the heaviness in my heart lighten a little bit more.

CHAPTER 9

With Mom's permission, Casey made me go back to her house for the afternoon so that we could catch up on all the developments. "We'll do homework, too," she promised Mom, who seemed relieved that I wouldn't be alone for hours while she and Grandma were gone.

"Does your mom know what Ethan did?" Casey whispered as we walked to Ben's truck, arm in arm. "We were all so worried when you didn't respond to any of our calls or texts last night and this morning, so we came over after church. We waited in the truck, though, when we saw that Daniel was already here. To give the two of you some time," she added mysteriously, then spoke in a louder voice. "By the way, we're not all going to fit in this truck. Not enough seat belts."

"I'll drive her to your house," Daniel said, overhearing since he was right behind us.

"Good, because you're coming over, too, Mr. Knight in Shining Armor." She spun around and touched his arm. "Everyone has heard about what you did, Batman. Well done."

"What do you mean by everyone?" I asked, frowning.

"Well, Ethan's friends can't keep a secret. Word gets around, and apparently those so-called friends want to distance themselves from this situation. They're bashing Ethan now and taking your side, Reese, even though they treated the post like a joke at the time."

She gave me a little side hug. "I think you'll find that everyone feels protective of you. When you go to school tomorrow, you'll have tons of support. Not a single person believes any of that nonsense Ethan wrote.

I do, I corrected her silently as I walked over to get in Daniel's car. Knowing that others might not be criticizing me was reassuring, though. Glancing over at Daniel's profile as he started the car, I acknowledged that having him take my side also lifted my spirits.

Even if our relationship never went any further, maybe he would still be my friend.

Daniel didn't linger long at Casey's house, saying he had chores and homework waiting at home. Plus, I knew his black eye had to be aching. He insisted on coming back in a few hours to drive me home, however, and I didn't argue, knowing it would give us a chance to talk in private.

"We have a plan," Mia announced once Daniel left. "Between the four of us and your other friends, we've got you covered so that you're never alone tomorrow at school."

I looked at her blankly, and Abby chimed in. "We don't know how Ethan is going to act around you, or how other kids who just want to create dumb drama might tease you, stuff like that. So, we'll be your bodyguards!"

"Well, not quite bodyguards," Casey corrected. "*Escorts* might be the better word, though Ben could take someone down if he had to. You'll always have someone with you in your classes, in the hallways, and at lunch. We've got your back."

"I'll wear my darkest sunglasses tomorrow," Ben informed me with a straight face. "And a black jacket. Going for the Secret Service look, you know."

"Hey, I could take someone down too," Mia said indignantly. "I may be short but I'm feisty!"

They all started laughing and joking around, but I just sat there in Casey's living room, taking in their words. They were going to *protect* me. Watch out for me. They didn't believe the worst of me.

I willed myself not to cry again, but a solitary tear escaped anyway, and Casey noticed. She scooted closer to me on the couch, wrapping an arm around my shoulders. "We love you, Reesie-poo."

"I don't deserve friends like you," I whispered, too grateful to object to the sappy nickname. There was that "deserve" word again. I didn't want to come across as some needy damsel in distress who needed constant reassurance, but I meant it.

"Of course you don't deserve us, honey," Casey teased. "But you're stuck with us anyway."

"That's right," Abby said staunchly, and she came over to give me a hug, too.

"Group hug!" Mia sang out, and Ben groaned.

"I'm out. See you tomorrow, Reese." Reaching in his pocket for his truck keys, he gave me a mock salute and then looked meaningfully at Casey.

"Go kiss your guy," I told her, giving her a little shove. "And thanks, Ben."

"Now," Mia said, rubbing her hands together. "Tell us all about Daniel. And what do your mom and grandma think about all of this?"

I groaned. That was yet another conversation to be dealt with. What *would* they think about all of this?

"My parents aren't happy about the fight, of course, but they're more upset about you."

Daniel had just driven me home, and we were sitting in his car, parked in the driveway. I had texted Mom to let her know I was here and would come inside in a few minutes.

His words made me go still. "They're upset with me?"

"No, *for* you. They're angry about Ethan's stupid stunt and worried that it might have hurt you. A physical hit usually heals up, but words?" His mouth was set in a grim line. "Words can scar you on the inside for a long, long time.

"On the bright side, my dad said I did the right thing by telling Ethan to take down the post, though he emphasized that a phone call would have been wiser." His expression became sheepish. "I have to say, though, it felt pretty good to hit him."

"In self-defense, of course," I clarified, and shook my head. "I'm so sorry that happened, Daniel. I need to go in and explain things to Mom now, but I'm okay. As you said earlier, I'm surrounded by friends."

Daniel looked at me steadily. I was distracted by his bruised eye, but even so I detected something different in his expression. What was it?

He took a deep breath. "Can I be honest, Reese?"

Okay, those words sent alarms sounding off in my head. "Um, sure?"

"I need to tell you how I feel about you."

Whoa. Those alarm bells clanged even louder. How he *felt* about me?

I stared at him uneasily, unable to look away. Was this where he would confirm what I had convinced myself of last night, that I was a hot mess and he needed to create some distance between us? Or maybe, possibly, that he was madly in love with me? Wild hope flared up in my heart, and I tamped it down firmly. That was ridicu-

"I care about you. You're an amazing person."

My heart soared again, though my stomach sank. I sat there, frozen. What should I do? This conversation could still go either way, right?

"I have feelings for you, Reese. I really want to get to know you better-"

Here it was. He was finally going to ask me out. I knew the drill, the lines, the routine. This amazing guy wanted to date me, and I wanted that too, I admitted that. But this script never worked for me. I had to cut him off. The whole vow thing.

"Daniel, I-"

"-but I don't want to be in a relationship right now. I don't want to be your boyfriend."

My eyes widened. For at least the second time that day, I was stunned into silence, and Daniel did nothing to rush any response. Settling back into his seat, he watched me carefully.

Wait. He had feelings for me and wanted to get to know me better, but he didn't want to be my boyfriend? He was not asking me on a date? What was this? Should I be offended? No boy had ever told Reese Owens he didn't want to date her! And yet, wasn't this exactly the status I was hoping for? Good friends and no more?

I should feel relieved that I didn't have to squelch my own growing attraction and lie to him, giving him the "let's just be friends" speech, allowing him to believe I was not interested in anything more. It stung, though. I was the one who always delivered that message, not the guy. I had *never* received that speech, only given it!

My mouth opened as I thought about replying one way,

then closed again as I changed my mind hastily, thinking of another way. Daniel noted my conflict, and that boy had the audacity to grin.

That did it. The ironic humor of the situation got the best of me, and I cracked a reluctant smile. "I should smack you, Dixon."

"Already been smacked." He snickered, and I tried to suppress a giggle, but it escaped anyway. He started chuckling, and with that we both lost it. We sat in that car laughing until our stomachs hurt, and there were tears in my eyes.

And that's how Mom found us when she walked outside "to water the flower bed" a few minutes later.

As I got ready for bed that night, I reflected on the difference that twenty-four hours could make. Last night I had cried myself to sleep, Daniel got in a fight on my account, my friends couldn't reach me and were worried, and I was convinced that I was an untrustworthy, fundamentally flawed person.

Tonight, my tears had resulted from laughter. My friends had come to find me even when I wouldn't communicate and were making plans to protect me. As for Daniel? We had turned a corner somehow. We were still in the friendship neighborhood, but he had let his guard down, admitting that he cared for me without seeming to expect anything at all. I didn't know what to make of that.

But I did know how all these things made me feel. Seen. Cared for.

I was still untrustworthy. All that inner turmoil was still entrenched in my mind. Yet, I knew there were people on my side.

"Thank you," I whispered, even while I didn't know who I

was whispering it to. Myself? Some unknown force in the universe?

Or maybe, possibly, to the God I kept hearing about at youth group? The one who supposedly knew me and loved me? Somehow, in this moment, that thought didn't seem so unreasonable.

I fell asleep as soon as my head hit the pillow.

CHAPTER 10

By lunch the next day I was very concerned, but not for me. True to their word, from the minute I parked my car at school my friends had never left me alone, and even students I didn't know were calling over as we passed each other in the halls, voicing support. I found some sticky notes on my locker with sweet messages written on them, and just now some members of the chess club had stopped by my lunch table, dropping off a plastic queen figure from a chess set with this note attached: "*We support you, Reese! Forever our queen!*"

I thanked them sincerely, feeling more than a bit awkward, but as soon as they went on their way I turned to Ben, who shared my lunch period and was currently on bodyguard duty. At least he hadn't worn his dark sunglasses.

"Seriously, I appreciate all this support so much, but you know what I've noticed? People are starting to bash Ethan. Won't *he* become the victim now? Like bullying in reverse?"

Ben frowned. "Don't worry about Ethan. What he did was wrong, and people don't like it. A message must be sent." He surveyed the large cafeteria. "Besides, he doesn't seem to be here today anyway." Ethan shared our lunch period, too.

Gulping down the rest of my veggie wrap, I gathered up my trash and stood up. "Well, I have to go to the counselor's office before my next class. Mom insisted on calling this morning to let her know what happened, and Ms. Guthrie asked me to come see her over lunch. You don't have to come with me, okay? I think I'm safe in her office!"

Ben stood up immediately. "Not happening. Casey will give me detention if I don't stick with you."

"Oh, so your true motivation is to stay in your girlfriend's good graces and not necessarily to protect me from the bad guys?" I teased him.

"Bingo." He finished his drink and picked up his tray. "Lead the way."

I was glad Ben was with me after all, when we entered the secretarial area outside the counselor offices. Ethan was slouched in a chair there, and as Daniel had told me, he definitely did not look pretty. Or happy.

If Daniel's left eye looked bad, Ethan's right one looked even worse. Noticing us walk in, he visibly tensed up. "Sheesh, man," Ben drawled. "Did you run into a brick wall?"

Before I could even guess his plan, Ben brushed ahead of me, advancing toward Ethan. Speaking in a low voice, his tone was grim. "Don't ever pull a stunt like that again."

The secretary looked our way, clearing her throat. "Have a seat, please. Are you Reese Owens, young lady? Ms. Guthrie is waiting for you, so go on in." She glared at Ben. "And *you* are?"

"Reese's friend, ma'am. I'll wait for her out here if you don't mind."

Keeping my expression blank, I looked away from Ethan and entered my counselor's office. I had absolute faith in that secretary's ability to keep both Ethan and Ben in line.

After giving her my version of the whole unfortunate experience, Ms. Guthrie watched me sympathetically. "How are you dealing with all of this?"

"I have a lot of support. I'm still upset with Ethan, but honestly, he's not a terrible person. I mean, what he did was horrible, but it's not typical for him. I don't think he's ever done anything like that before." I hesitated as the memory of Ethan's stiffness toward me at the prom came to mind. "I disappointed him, and... and maybe I deserved it. His anger, I mean, not the way he expressed it with that awful post."

"We must all learn to manage strong emotions in healthy ways," Ms. Guthrie said slowly. "Just keep in mind, Reese, that you are not responsible for Ethan's behavior in any way. Even if you disappoint or anger him, or anyone else for that matter, it does not mean you should accept cruelty or abuse as some sort of punishment."

"I know." Ms. Guthrie waited, and when I didn't say anything else, she cleared her throat.

"Moving forward," she said, more business-like now. "Even though this incident happened off campus, anti-bullying laws are in place that allow our school to consider disciplinary action, which will be decided on soon. I spoke with your mother earlier about the option of obtaining a restraining order." She went on to talk about the definition of bullying and such, but my mind zeroed in on just two of her words.

Restraining order? Wasn't that way over the top?

By the time our meeting ended, there were only two minutes left to get to my next class, but to his credit Ben was still waiting for me outside of Ms. Guthrie's office. Fortunately, we had the same Algebra class next period.

"Let's hustle!" I urged, and Ben didn't waste a minute, hitching his backpack over his shoulder. I paused only long enough to glance at Ethan, still sitting in the same chair, and his eyes met mine briefly. Somehow, it didn't surprise me to see that his expression matched the look I had worn on my own face, this past Saturday night.

He looked wretched.

Ethan wasn't at school on Tuesday, and word on the street was that he had been suspended for the day. Even so, my friends decided to keep up the bodyguard act all that week, "just in case." The football buddies who had been drinking at Ethan's house with him on Saturday were still around, and Casey thought they might bother me somehow.

As it turned out, they did bother me but not at all in a threatening way. If anything, they were all Team Reese, and went out of their way to trash Ethan. At lunch, a couple of them came over to my table to specifically say hi and ask how I was doing since "Ethan was such a jerk." Another one in my Spanish class put a nice little note on my desk with a peppermint candy. I threw them both away and ignored the other attempts to "check on me." By Thursday, though, I was fed up.

"Incoming," Ben murmured as we sat at our usual table outside during lunch, enjoying the sunny, mild weather. Ethan's two football buddies who shared our lunch period were heading our way, looking all serious and concerned. I groaned and that's when, as Grandma would say, "the spirit of slap" came over me.

Standing up, I crossed my arms and faced the two jocks, enjoying how their expressions changed from confidence to slight uneasiness. Still, one of them tried.

"You doin' okay, Reese?" he said, as if he was talking to a sick ten-year-old.

"Better than you," I snapped, and he looked surprised. That's when Buddy #2 had a go.

"Is anything wrong? Just say what you need, and we're here for you."

Ben snickered, and both guys looked at him in confusion. Shaking his head, Ben calmly took a bite of his sloppy joe.

"As a matter of fact," I said coolly, enunciating every single word, "I could have used your help on Saturday night. Where were you when Ethan posted that vile comment about me? Tell me."

Both guys shifted their feet. "It wasn't our idea."

"We told him it was dumb. Ethan's an idiot," the other guy said defensively.

"And *yet*," I responded, popping that "t" at the end of *yet*. "You were complicit. Not only that, here you are acting all innocent and stabbing your own friend in the back." I extended an arm now, pointing dramatically, not to anything in particular but just for effect. "Begone!"

They left, slinking off in a hurry, heading for anywhere that wasn't near me. And with that, everyone at my lunch table started clapping, slowly at first, and then whistling and cheering. Students at other tables who had overheard the whole thing joined in.

It was a fine moment, and I gave a little mock curtsy.

"You did great, Reese," Ben praised me a few minutes later as we gathered up our trash to get to the next class. "But seriously? *Begone*?"

"I've waited my whole life to use that word in a sentence," I confided, and then we both cracked up.

CHAPTER 11

After their initial gasps and outrage, Mom and Grandma were surprisingly calm about the whole Ethan situation. We discussed the restraining order idea, but I convinced them that my gut told me Ethan's behavior was a one-off impulsive act that he probably regretted.

"Has he apologized yet?" Mom would ask each night at dinner, and each time the answer was no. This Thursday evening, however, I added a possible explanation.

"Daniel told me that Ethan may have been instructed not to talk to me or communicate with me at all."

"Daniel, yes," Grandma murmured. "I like that young man. Is he planning a career in law?"

I shrugged. "I don't know. His uncle probably mentioned the possibility since he's a police officer. Speaking of that – "

I chose my next words carefully, thinking while I took a sip of iced tea. "I'm meeting with Daniel and his uncle tomorrow after school at Daniel's house, if that's okay. Daniel wants me to ask his uncle Danny any questions I might have about the situation. Not that I have any- I don't- but he might have some good advice. I'll be back in plenty of time to help at the rehearsal dinner at seven, don't worry! It's going to be fancy, right? I remember it's a Bless Their Hearts wedding, so we'll have our hands full, won't we?"

My perky change of subject worked on Grandma, who immediately started telling me about the latest unexpected demand, this time from the groom's mother. Mom, however, was noticeably quiet for the rest of the meal, and didn't eat much.

"Reese, honey," she called, after the dishes were cleared away and I was starting back upstairs to go study. The big AP History exam was tomorrow morning at 8 A.M. sharp.

I paused, already a couple of steps up the staircase. "Yes, ma'am?"

Mom looked up at me with concern in her eyes that almost looked like fear. I took a step back down. "Mom, you know I'm okay, right? I'm fine. You don't need to worry about the incident with Ethan anymore."

Her expression softened. "I hope that proves to be true, Reese. I do want us to talk over everything before the weekend is over, okay? I need a pulse check." This was her code for *I want you to tell me every single detail that's going on in your life right now*, and I smiled at her reassuringly.

"Sure, we'll talk. I'll tell you *all* the things I choose to let you know." This was my usual teasing response, and Mom would always roll her eyes and give me a little fake swat. This time, however, she had more to say.

"There is something else I want to discuss. Not emergency stuff, just- there are things we should talk about." She swallowed. "Now go study. You're going to ace that test tomorrow, my smart girl."

Leaning over to give her a quick hug, I headed up the stairs, my mind already on the meeting tomorrow with Daniel and certainly not on U.S. History. Yes, Daniel's uncle would be there for a few minutes before he went on his shift. That was true. The main purpose of me going to Daniel's house, however, was just to hang out for a while, like friends do. Daniel had asked if we could get to know each other better, on a non-date.

"There will be snacks," he promised this morning with a gleam in his eye, and I had laughed and immediately agreed, squelching all misgivings my brain threw at me.

After all, Daniel's mom would also be there the entire time. All the conditions of my no dating vow were being met, right? It was a strange set-up, like a kid's play date, but I was looking forward to it.

A lot.

At the top of the stairs, I sensed Mom still watching me because I turned slightly and there she was, looking up from the bottom.

This time, though, she looked sad.

About an hour after school the next day, I rang Daniel's doorbell. He opened the front door immediately, greeting me with a mock frown. "You're seven seconds late," he scolded. "I should tell you to *begone*."

"You heard about that?" I drawled, passing him to enter the living room.

"Are you kidding? It's all over school. Reese Owens is a legend."

I rolled my eyes. "It was a high price to pay for legendary status, but I'll take it. Here, Casey said you like these." I held out a bag of sour gummy bears.

"A legend who brings me gummy bears? How will I ever resist you, Reese?" His words were said jokingly, but I stiffened anyway. I had to, or else I would absolutely melt into a puddle at the warm look in his eyes.

He changed the subject quickly. "Come meet my Uncle Danny, in the kitchen. And thanks for the gummies. Casey bribed me with them to help her out earlier this year."

Following him to the kitchen, I attempted to lighten things up. "Yeah, about that. I want to hear all about these bargains you two made in history class." He laughed and gestured to a handsome man in a police uniform, standing by the sink and talking to Mrs. Dixon.

"Uncle Danny, this is my friend Reese. Reese, meet one of our city's finest, the original Daniel Dixon. I was named after him in case you're wondering."

I smiled and nodded. "Nice to meet you, officer." I waited, we all waited, for Daniel's uncle to respond, like polite people do. But he didn't. He just stood there, staring at me in shock like I was a ghost.

"Danny?" Mrs. Dixon gave him a curious glance but walked over to give me a hug. "So nice to see you again, Reese. I'm furious about what happened to you, but Daniel says you're managing things like a champ."

"I've had tons of support," I told her. "Otherwise, it would be a different story, I'm sure."

By then, Uncle Danny had found his manners. "Nice to meet you too, Reese. Sorry about that, you just, uhh... I didn't catch your last name but let me guess. Would it happen to be Owens? Are you by chance related to Ruby Owens?"

Surprised, I looked at Daniel, but he was watching his uncle intently. "Yes, sir," I responded. "Ruby is my mother."

"How did you know that?" Daniel demanded, and Uncle Danny answered his question while looking at me, his face unreadable.

"Ruby and I went to high school together. You look exactly

like your mother, and when you walked in it was like seeing Ruby all over again. Like she was frozen in time," he said in a weak attempt at humor, but nobody laughed.

This wasn't that unusual, I reminded myself. I did look exactly like Mom. She had grown up in this town and attended another high school here, though she missed her senior year when she became pregnant with me. She hadn't kept in touch with any of her high school friends, as far as I knew. Had Danny been a friend, or.... more? Maybe an ex-boyfriend? Did he know... was he possibly... but Mom would surely have said something...

My heart started beating faster, my eyes locked with his. This original Daniel Dixon had known my mother when she was my age. Maybe I should talk to him? Privately. Now? No, I was here to get advice. Cyberbullying, right? Would talking to him be going behind Mom's back? Would she mind? He had to go to work soon. Was I making a big deal out of nothing? *What should I do?*

All senses on high alert, my mind raced even faster than my heart rate, my thoughts jumbled together. Agitation must have shown on my face because Daniel and his mom looked at each other in some kind of silent communication, and Daniel touched my shoulder gently. "Let's go outside on the back porch for a minute, okay?"

I followed him numbly, tearing my gaze away from Uncle Danny. When we stepped out onto the back porch, I heard Mrs. Dixon begin talking to him in a low voice, though I couldn't make out the words. Daniel closed the door behind us firmly and led me to a white wicker chair, padded with blue patterned cushions. "Sit. Breathe."

I sank down in the chair, and Daniel sat down in another one next to mine, his long legs sprawled out in front of him. We sat quietly, watching the birds at a feeder several yards away, or at least Daniel did. I just stared in that direction blankly, not really seeing anything until the whirlwind of thoughts that had hijacked my brain slowed down. The busy chirping of the birds finally registered, and I looked around.

This large backyard was fenced but behind it there was nothing but trees, like Grandma's backyard. Raised flowerbeds contained rosebushes of all colors, blooming profusely, and there were two tall trees providing some shade.

Taking deep breaths, my heart rate slowed back down to normal, my mind became calmer, and my thoughts grew less chaotic. A bird sang its heart out in one of the trees, and I broke our silence. "What kind of bird is that, singing?"

"A northern mockingbird. He's a noisy guy and sometimes keeps other birds away from the feeder, even though he doesn't eat there himself. He's annoying like me, so I like him. I'm sure you recognize the bluejay." He started identifying a few of the other birds. I listened absently, liking the deep sound of his voice and glad for the distraction of his words, his company. Obviously, Daniel recognized how flustered I had become when his uncle told me he knew my mother. And once again he came to my rescue, this time by quietly giving me a place to regain my composure.

"Gummies?" he offered, holding out the bag he was still carrying.

I managed a smile. "Sure. I like the blue ones."

"Noted." He opened the bag, and we continued sitting, sharing gummy bears, and watching the birds. I finally sighed, shaking my head in frustration.

"Sorry I came unglued in there. Your uncle probably thinks I'm some fragile, unstable"-

"Whoa, stop right there, Reese. Uncle Danny meets fragile, unstable people all the time in his job, and I don't think you would qualify. For what it's worth, though, he acted pretty flustered, too. I've never seen him look like that when he met you. Ever."

He hesitated, then went on. "Also, for what it's worth, we don't have to talk about this. That's part of the deal as friends. We'll be honest with each other, but some subjects can be off limits. You agree?"

I turned in my chair to face him fully. There he went again, giving me privacy and support with no expectations, no pressure. I made up my mind. "I do agree, but I will talk to you about *this*. And I'd like to talk to your uncle again. Just not right now," I added hastily, checking the large kitchen window which faced the backyard.

"Don't worry, I think he's left already." Daniel shrugged. "We'll set up another meeting with him whenever you want."

I was determined to get the next few words out, specifically the one word I rarely spoke. "Daniel?" He looked at me steadily, giving me his undivided attention.

"Your uncle might have known my father. I don't know who my father *is*. I've never even been that curious, but now, meeting your uncle, well..." I looked down at my hands, clenched tightly together. "I guess I'm curious now."

The words were spoken clearly, with no wobble in my voice, and I counted that as a small victory. Even so, Daniel reached his hand out, wiggling his fingers at me as he had done before, inviting me to take it and hold on. I did, without any hesitation.

I held on tight.

CHAPTER 12

Getting home about an hour later, I heard Mom and Grandma talking in our office, separated from the living room by elegant French doors. Every now and then they would meet with clients there, but mostly the room was the base of operations for Your Perfect Day, where all the "magic" happened. The endless spreadsheets, phone calls, timelines, and website updates, basically managing a thousand details so that the bride could have her worry-free day, sure didn't seem magical on our end. It was a ton - no, *ten* tons of work during busy seasons.

Even so, at the end of every single event that I had helped with so far, I felt proud and gratified to see the happiness on the faces of the bridal couple, or whoever the event was organized for. I knew I could take a tiny bit of credit for it, and that's when I personally felt the magic.

Tonight, though, was all about avoidance.

Daniel had helped me calm down, but just as I wanted to gather my thoughts before speaking again to his uncle, I also needed some time to figure out how I felt about Mom. We were close, a "me and you against the world" team for my whole life, but people who are close don't keep big secrets. Or do they? Why did Mom rarely mention my father?

To be fair, I had hardly ever brought up the whole daddy issue either. Why not? Wasn't that something a well-adjusted, rational young woman would do? It's not like I never wondered about who, or where, he was. With every daddy-daughter dance, each birthday, and obviously any time I saw a bride being walked down the aisle by her father, I felt a bit cheated. Why couldn't I be that girl with the loving dad? I had accepted it all these years, though. Lots of girls didn't have dads, or moms. It's the way things were, and I didn't lose any sleep over it.

But now? Meeting someone who knew my mom in high school, and therefore might have known my dad? The tiny suspicion that Uncle Danny could even *be* my dad was freaking me out right now. Absolutely not. No. Way! If that were true, Mom would surely have known this and never let me go over to the Dixon house unprepared. I chose to believe this.

I felt frustrated with Mom, I didn't even understand my *own* brain, and we still had a job to do tonight. There was no time for a heart-to-heart conversation, or a personal meltdown.

Therefore, avoidance.

"I'm home and going upstairs to get ready," I called out in the direction of the office and hurried off, not waiting for any reply. Taking my time once my bedroom door was closed, I took a shower, got dressed and played with my makeup until the very last possible minute, right before we had to leave. I then walked cautiously downstairs where Grandma was already waiting.

"It's just you and me, Reese," she informed me. "Your mother has a headache, and we don't need three people at this event anyway."

Perfect! I smiled in sheer relief, and Grandma looked at me oddly. "We've got this, Grandma!" I told her with forced cheerfulness. "Hope Mom feels better soon." Who knows, maybe Mom was avoiding me too.

But hey, after years of ignoring a subject, what was one more day?

As it turned out, Mom was truly sick and running a fever by the time we got home that night, and Grandma insisted that she stay in bed the next day. On the one hand this was quite a relief, given that I was allergic to Mom's company right now, though of course I didn't want her to be sick. On the other hand, it put Grandma in a bind. Your Perfect Day was booked this weekend, with two weddings on Saturday and an anniversary reception on Sunday afternoon.

I found Grandma in our office Saturday morning, scowling at the computer screen. "You're up early, dear," she commented. "I hope you're not coming down with whatever your mother has?"

"Nope, I'm fine," I told her. "I'm reporting for duty. I'll be Mom today."

Grandma glared at me over her reading glasses. "Absolutely not," she said firmly. "This is your study weekend. You have finals next week. Don't you have another study session scheduled with your friends this afternoon?"

I shrugged. "Meh, I don't have to be there. I'll study tomorrow from dawn to dusk, I promise. I'm fairly caught up anyway, since two of my classes required final projects instead of exams, which I've already completed. Besides..."

I walked over to the white antique desk where she was sitting and put my arm around her, bending over to give her a little kiss on the top of her head. "If I'm not your assistant today then who *will* be? I know you have choices, of course. There's

Francine at the top of the list, and of course you can always hit up Mrs. Vandever."

I felt Grandma shudder and smiled. Francine was Grandma's best friend, who she loved dearly, but they were total opposites. While Grandma was a brisk Type A personality, driven and precise, Francine was the artsy type who floated through her days, spreading happiness wherever she went but shaky with handling details.

Mrs. Vandever, on the other hand, was Grandma's unofficial arch enemy. Also an event planner, she contracted exclusively with a fancy venue in our town, a gig which Grandma coveted. She and Grandma did help each other from time to time as a professional courtesy, though Grandma swore Mrs. Vandever loaned her the most incompetent people on purpose.

Knowing this would clinch the deal, I made my next remarks sound casual. "The afternoon garden wedding is a Bless Their Hearts couple, right? And the wedding tonight is rustic, in a barn? With the big barbeque menu and country band? I guess Francine could handle all of that." I allowed my voice to trail away.

Grandma heaved an exasperated sigh, took off her glasses, and rubbed her temples with her fingers. "Enough, Reese. Can you be ready to leave by ten a.m.?"

I squeezed her shoulders. "Done. I do expect a great big bonus in my first paycheck, of course."

Always the businesswoman, Grandma chuckled, her eyes gleaming with appreciation. "We'll negotiate that later, dear. Now, after this weekend is over my very first priority is to find another reliable backup if you and Ruby are ever unavailable at the same time. Just imagine... Francine *indeed*..."

I left her muttering to herself and went to find us a quick breakfast.

> How's it going, legend? Need some
> gummies?

Daniel's text was a welcome break from what had been an exhausting, busy-to-the-max weekend. Here it was, only three o'clock on Sunday afternoon, and I was ready to go to bed already, with at least another hour of studying to do.

> I'm not the gummy fanatic you are, but what
> I wouldn't give for a frappuccino!

His response was instant.

> Text me exactly what you want and I'll be
> there in 20.

I shook my head, though I was alone here in my bedroom. I hadn't meant my words as a hint. He didn't have to go to all that trouble! I mean, yeah, I sure could use a frap but I could grab some keys and go get one myself. While I was still deliberating, his next text came through.

> I'm getting one for me, so I might as well get
> one for you. Delivered to your door, no
> problem.

There was never really any doubt that I would cave in, so I texted him my order. There was also no question that even more than the caffeine, the thought of seeing Daniel Dixon again for just five minutes made me feel fully revived and totally awake.

Thirty minutes later, we were sipping our coffees in the kitchen and talking. I told him about my Saturday, how Grandma was working this afternoon's event alone and that Mom had been sick but was now fever-free, watching TV in the living room. He told me about the study session I missed yesterday and the summer job he had applied for. Sometimes we were both quiet, but it was never awkward. I didn't feel like I needed to keep the conversation going just to be sociable; it was okay to sit together quietly. To just exist. I contemplated this as I took my last sip of coffee, enjoying the thought.

"I'd better let you get back to Algebra," Daniel finally said. He didn't move a muscle, though.

"Physics," I corrected him. "Algebra is conquered. And my Physics final is not until Wednesday so I may just call it an early night and make up for it tomorrow. It's my hardest subject," I admitted.

"Good plan. Hey, Uncle Danny told me to give you a message." The change of subject was abrupt, but Daniel still seemed relaxed, so it was probably no big deal. My nerves tensed up anyway.

"You didn't tell him about my dad, right? Or lack of one?"

"Of course not." Daniel looked insulted. "I would never betray your confidence, Reese."

"I believe you," I reassured him hastily. "Sorry, I know that. So, what's the message?"

"He said to tell you, and I quote, 'You're beautiful like your mom although I don't want that to come across as creepy.'" I smiled and Daniel went on. "He said your mom was his friend and he missed her when she went to another school before her senior year. He'll be glad to talk to you anytime when you're both free."

"Okay, that's a nice message," I said slowly. "Does he know that Mom went out of state, and not just to another high school here in town? Does he know that she was pregnant with me?" I had told Daniel some of our history the other day while we sat in his backyard.

"He won't know a single thing unless you tell him," Daniel said firmly. "It's not my story. He can do the math though,

68

right? You're seventeen, and he and your mom are the same age, so he knows you were born when *she* was seventeen." He paused. "I did ask him a question, Reese, and I hope you don't mind. I wanted to know if he and your mom were more than just friends, if they ever dated. I – I really needed to know this myself."

I caught my breath. *Dear God, here it is. Please help me.* I didn't stop to analyze why I was praying to a God I wasn't sure was there. Searching Daniel's face, I looked for a hint of good news, though I also wasn't entirely sure what that good news would be.

"Just tell me," I whispered.

"They never dated, never had a romantic relationship. He said he had a big crush on her, but they were never anything more than casual friends."

I sagged in my chair in what I recognized as relief, closing my eyes. Daniel's uncle was not my dad. *Thank you.* When I opened my eyes again I smiled at Daniel, but his attention was no longer on me, and he looked intensely uncomfortable.

Oh, no. Turning around in my chair, I followed Daniel's gaze. And there was Mom, wearing her robe and looking like a teenager herself with her hair in a ponytail and no makeup, standing in the kitchen archway and looking stricken.

CHAPTER 13

"We don't have to do this right now, Mom."

She and I were sitting on her bed, both leaning back on fluffy pillows propped against the headboard. Daniel had left soon after Mom overheard the last part of our conversation in the kitchen, and Grandma would be home any minute from the reception. Mom had insisted, however, that she and I needed to talk. Now. Privately.

She didn't answer me right away, so I went on, doggedly. "I mean, you've been sick, I'm super tired, and we both need to get to bed soon." There. I had given Mom an excuse to delay this conversation if she wanted it. An out. A logical reason for avoidance. Part of me desperately wanted her to back out, but an even bigger part was now so preoccupied with all things "father" that I didn't think I would ever sleep again until I had some answers.

"No, Reese, it's time. *Past* time. I still want to do a pulse check with you about the Ethan situation, but let's get the elephant out of the room first. The one that's been there for years." To my surprise, there was a hint of dry humor in her tone, and I responded in kind.

"Is this particular elephant a male? A daddy elephant?"

"That's the one. I've practiced this conversation in my head for years, but I've only actually planned for it in the last couple of weeks. I wanted to wait until school was out for the summer and you didn't have so much on your mind, but now?"

"Now is the time," I finished for her, realizing that it was true. Would there ever be a perfect time for this conversation? Maybe. But neither Mom nor I were experts in perfection, so why wait?

"Now," Mom repeated. She gave a decisive nod, looking a lot like Grandma in that moment, then reached over to her bedside table, picked up a book and handed it to me.

It was a large, though thin, rectangular book, with several sticky notes attached to some pages. On the front was the title "Bonham High School."

"This is your high school yearbook?" I whispered, staring at the book in my hands, and my heart started pounding again. Bonham was the largest and oldest high school in our town. My own high school, Rayburn, was built only about ten years ago, to meet the growing demand for another high school in our area.

"From my junior year," Mom affirmed. "I was your age. I marked the pages that have pictures of your father."

My father.

Hands trembling, I turned to the first page marked with a sticky note, opening the yearbook like it was a sacred relic that would crumble if I was too rough with it. Staring at the rows of photographs on the pages before me, I remembered I didn't know my father's name.

"Which one is he?" I asked, still whispering.

"You have his smile. I thought maybe you could guess which one he is. But here, I'll point him out." And she did.

I looked at the blond teenage boy in the picture, so

handsome with a self-assured smile, and started to cry, silent tears that streamed down my cheeks. *This is my father. Joshua Lockwood.* I repeated the name silently, over and over, memorizing it in my heart.

I studied his face, his features, trying to see my own smile reflected in his, like Mom had said. I would have to study my smile in a mirror. Turning to the next marked page, I was suddenly hungry to learn everything I possibly could about this boy, now a man. "He played football," I breathed, noting the uniform he wore. "What position?"

Mom answered my questions one after another, coming faster as I turned the pages. He played defense and was also on the track and field team. There was a picture of him dressed like a cheerleader for a fundraiser powder puff game, performing a halftime routine with the other guys and looking ridiculous. Josh had a great sense of humor, Mom told me, and was always laughing.

I came to a casual group photo including him and a girl who looked just like me. They were obviously at a formal dance, their arms around each other and wearing wide, carefree smiles. "Homecoming," Mom told me. "I still remember how happy we were that night."

I went still. "You were in love, then."

Mom's voice was steady. "We did love each other, at least as much as we understood what love was at that time. It was all feelings, though. And while feelings are important, love is more than just feelings. True love is a decision, a decision you make every day."

"A decision you were too young to make, right?" My mind flew to my own experiences with boys I thought I had loved. We had all the feelings too, just like Mom said, but those relationships turned out to be shaky. They fell apart.

Mom looked thoughtful. "Actually, I think our relationship

could have made it if we had understood then what real love was all about. True love doesn't give up. It's patient and kind, it protects and perseveres."

I turned and stared at Mom, amazed. "What you just said... that's from the Bible."

"Yes!" Mom nodded. "So, you've read it before?"

"Casey wrote some verses down and gave them to me this year." I hesitated. "It's a long story."

"Well, I want to hear it, but tonight is about your father," Mom said, seeming determined to keep us on track. "What else do you want to know?"

I sat up straighter. "Mom, does Joshua Lockwood know I even exist? Did he abandon you and me? Is he still alive, and if so, where is he?"

Grandma knocked on our door a few minutes later to check on us, but we didn't invite her into our conversation, and she didn't ask any questions, saying that she was tired and turning in early. That led me to another whole subset of questions- how had Grandma reacted seventeen years ago? Did she know where my father was? Did she know his parents? My other *grandparents*?

Mom and I talked for only about another half hour before I started to feel completely overwhelmed and exhausted. Most of my questions were still unanswered, but I needed to process everything I had already learned before I could take on even one more detail.

Two texts came within seconds of each other, as I brushed my teeth a bit later. The first one was expected.

Are you and your mom okay?

I smiled to myself, grateful for Daniel's concern.

> I think so. LOTS to tell you later. Too tired now.

He responded with a thumbs up and his usual "**sweet dreams, Reese**."

The second text was quite unexpected.

> Can we talk?

My smile actually widened as the irony of the situation hit me. If I had received this message earlier this morning I would have obsessed about it all day, wondering how I should respond. It would have raised my stress levels. But now? The message barely registered, competing with the other new information about my father fresh in my mind.

This text was from Ethan.

I turned off my phone and went to bed, where I tossed and turned all night.

CHAPTER 14

It was Monday morning, the first day of finals week, I had overslept and had to rush to get to school on time, and I was still emotionally exhausted from the big dad reveal. So the very *last* thing I needed was to see a familiar young man waiting by my locker.

"Reese, you didn't answer my text. Can we talk soon, like today?"

I ignored Ethan while I quickly stowed the books I didn't need into my locker. Only three of our classes met today, for longer sessions than usual, and I had a final exam in the last one. Slamming the locker door, I finally looked at him directly, halfway wishing my self-appointed bodyguard crew had decided to shadow me for an extra week.

"Not today, Ethan. Gotta run." I started walking down the hall to my first class, but I did call back a comment to him over my shoulder. "That eye still looks sick." In a hurry, I didn't notice the tall, broad-shouldered guy about to pass me until the last minute.

With one look at his face, however, grim and laser-focused

on Ethan, I grabbed him by the arm, tugging him around. "You already have one black eye, Dixon. Let's roll."

"He shouldn't be hanging around your locker. Is he that dumb?" Daniel muttered all the way to the end of the hallway, where we had to part ways and head in different directions.

He must have alerted Ben because when I finally made it to my usual table outside at lunch, still running a bit late, there Ben was, sitting with my other friends. "Shoo!" I told him. "Be free and go sit with your usual crew. I'll be fine."

"These ladies are my friends, too," he answered, sounding injured. He looked around the table for support, and the ladies giggled.

"You bet!" my friend Leah agreed. "Hey Reese, I heard that Ethan wants to talk to you, which could be a good thing, but I would be careful. He's right over there and I think he's been waiting for you."

I rolled my eyes. "How does everyone at Rayburn always know my business?" *Well, not all my business,* I added mentally. The information about my father was still very much on my mind, but there were only certain people I would discuss that with, and they were not sitting at my table right now.

Leah nudged me playfully. "We're just looking out for you, Reesie. But hey." She lowered her voice. "Don't talk to him alone, okay?"

Taking a drink from my water bottle, I then unwrapped the granola bar I had grabbed that morning before rushing out the door. "Y'all, Ethan acted like a jerk but he's not a monster, okay? He's not going to hurt me, and I'll bet he's sorry for what he did."

"She's right."

Leah stiffened and Ben narrowed his eyes at Ethan, standing behind me. I swallowed the bite of granola I had managed to take and braced myself.

"Can we talk privately, Reese? For just a few minutes?"

I was so tired. Mouthing an "I've got this" to Ben, who was now glaring at *me*, I turned around on the bench to face Ethan, deciding to use one of Grandma's delay and deflect tactics.

Well, almost. The first part of that strategy was to smile sweetly, and I was just too plain exhausted for that. Parts two and three were delivered seamlessly, however. I paused like I was thinking, and then responded. "I'll need some time to think about that. I'll let you know." Meeting his eyes briefly, I turned back around in my seat and took another bite of granola bar.

There was silence at my table, and I heard nothing more from Ethan, who apparently retreated. What else could he do? If he became insistent, it would make him look bad.

Ben looked amused. "How do you *do* that? You should be a diplomat."

I lifted one shoulder in a shrug, and Leah gave me a little side hug. "Well done! But still, watch your back."

I conceded and decided she was right. After I spoke to Ethan just now, I had seen a flash of frustration, or possibly anger, on his face. Even though I had defended him, I agreed with Leah. It wouldn't hurt to be careful.

I would watch my back.

The rest of finals week trudged along slowly. In addition to studying, Mom and I talked privately each night after dinner, just the two of us. She answered every question I asked and yet with every word she spoke, curiosity about my father kept growing, like a long-dormant seed just now receiving the rain it needed to sprout.

Our shortest conversation, however, was the hardest.

It was Thursday night, and we were again propped up with pillows on Mom's bed. "When I saw that Josh was cheating on me that afternoon, I was angry and devastated." Mom's voice was reflective. "But looking back, it was the reality check I needed to realize that he wasn't going to do some grand gesture like marry me. When I broke up with him a few days later, I only told him I knew he had cheated, and I wanted nothing more to do with him. I expected him to look guilty, and he did, but I'll never forget the other look on his face. It was relief." She sighed. "He wasn't even close to thinking about becoming a husband, much less a father."

"Well, you weren't ready to be a wife and mother, either, so that's hardly fair," I pointed out. "He was equally responsible. Why didn't you tell him about me, and at least give him a chance to respond? That wasn't right, Mom. It wasn't fair to him to not even know he had a child, it wasn't fair to you, and it especially wasn't fair to me." My tone was sharp.

There. I hadn't planned on saying those words yet, simmering under the surface ever since I was told Joshua Lockwood didn't know about me, but there was no point in delaying them any longer. Mom's solitary decision to cut my father out of my life before he even had the chance to know I existed, had affected each of our histories, especially mine. I let my words sit, heavy with accusation, and Mom did not rush to respond.

In the strained silence another thought made my stomach sink. My relationship with Mom had always been tight, but would this revelation change that? Mom had been dishonest with me. Maybe she hadn't technically lied, but information was withheld that I was entitled to have. How could our trust, our closeness, remain the same if it even survived? I didn't see how it could, and along with the slow burning anger another emotion began to emerge.

Loss. Crossing my arms, I hugged myself tightly, as if I was cold.

Mom finally spoke. "Reese, for so many years I convinced myself that I made the right decision, for all of us. I didn't want to have any more ties with Josh. I knew we didn't have a future together as a couple, so I determined that I would go it alone." She hesitated.

"In my mind I thought I was making the best decision. Josh could go on with his life, and I would go on with mine. Or *our* lives, that is. I also thought that Josh would want me to end the pregnancy if he knew about it." She touched my arm, but I pulled away. "It wasn't fair to assume that. Looking back, it was all about me, what I wanted, what I thought was right. I was proud. Angry. Selfish."

Mom sat up straight on the bed and turned to face me. "Look at me, Reese." Her commanding tone took me by surprise, and years of being taught respect for my elders caused me to automatically, though reluctantly, obey.

Her eyes held the sheen of tears, but her voice was steady. "I'm sorry, baby. I thought my decision was the best thing for me and you. Though it seemed right at the time, it was wrong of me. My decisions impacted you in a huge way. But going forward, I will help you in any way I can. If you want to contact your father, I will support you every step of the way."

My decisions impacted you.

In a flash, my own epic fails came to mind. My past mistakes, including hurting Ethan... how was I any better than Mom, at seventeen? I had been hurt, too, but I had done my own share of damage to other people.

Watching my face, Mom waited for my response. Slowly, I edged over to the side of her bed and stood up, the mixture of anger, guilt and grief making me crave the privacy of my own room. As I opened her door, I looked back and watched Mom's concern turn to sad resignation.

I left, shutting the door behind me.

CHAPTER 15

"Steer- *ike*!"

"Are you always this obnoxious, Dixon? Why yes, yes you are," Casey joked as we all observed Daniel showing off his bowling skills, making his third strike in a row.

Finals week was over and at least half of Rayburn High's junior class had taken over the bowling lanes this Friday night. Tomorrow was graduation, so this was also an impromptu celebration of the fact that we were almost officially seniors.

"I'm glad I'm on your team, Daniel," another girl cooed, someone I didn't know very well but who had asked if she could join our group. She kept batting her fake eyelashes at him. My hackles went up something fierce, but Daniel just grinned at her as he walked back to where our team was sitting.

"As you should be," he responded to her cockily, then plopped down in the chair beside me. Taking my hand, he kissed the back of it right in front of everyone, holding my gaze the entire time.

My hackles went down, but I pulled my hand away. "What was that?" I hissed, leaning over like I was whispering a sweet nothing into his ear.

"Just sending a message," he whispered right back, his face so close to mine that I shivered, settling back in my chair quickly. *Don't look at him,* I told myself, but of course I did anyway. Daniel winked at me, his eyes full of glee, and for some reason that made me relax.

"You're up!" Casey nudged me, and I took my mediocre bowling skills, found the ball I had been using, and positioned myself to try to get it down the lane.

"Want some tips, legend?" Daniel said right behind me, and I jumped.

"What is wrong with you tonight? Are you *flirting* with me?" I kept my voice low, turning around slightly. Honestly, was he trying to attract everyone's attention? What happened to our friend zone thing?

Daniel looked genuinely surprised. "I don't know, am I? Is this flirting? Maybe the hand kiss was over the top, but I just wanted that girl to know that I'm interested in you, not her."

"Oh. Okay. Well." I was breathless.

"Any day now!" someone from the other team called out. "Take your turn already!"

Daniel grinned and spun around to stroll back to his seat. I watched him, also noticing the knowing smirk Casey was giving me, and then pivoted back to focus on those pins I was supposed to knock down.

Stiffen your spine, girl. As that thought came, another followed immediately. Words that Mom had spoken to me as I left the house tonight, though I barely acknowledged them or her either. *Relax and have some fun.*

Squaring my shoulders, I gave it all I had and then watched as my gutter ball made its way slowly, slowly to the end of the lane. That's all it took. Something shifted in me, after my own personal gutter ball of a week.

I found myself smiling, picturing the happiness on Daniel's

face tonight, and decided to join whatever private party he was having. For the next few hours, I would forget algebra, physics, confusing mom and dad stuff, and the self-reproach that always lurked just under the surface. I would allow myself to have some fun.

Later, gathered with friends at our favorite, crowded pizza place, Daniel made sure to sit next to me. "We need to catch up," he murmured, leaning in close. "You have things to tell me."

"I sure do," I agreed, shivering again as I felt his breath on my ear. "But when? Are you going to graduation tomorrow afternoon? I'm sitting with Casey's family, since her stepbrother Jackson is graduating."

"I'm going, but I'll be sitting with the basketball team to support our seniors. So how about breakfast tomorrow? I know a good diner, though it can get noisy."

In the end, we decided he would go through a drive-through to get breakfast burritos, and then meet up with me at a park. Casey noticed all our whispering, of course, raising her eyebrows at me, and I felt guilty. There was so much I hadn't told her, and she needed updates, too. Should I invite her to our breakfast in the park? Daniel wouldn't mind since it wasn't a date, after all. We were just two friends meeting to talk. As it should be. I was content with that since friendship was all I wanted as well. Right?

Daniel turned around to grin at me, like I was the only one in the restaurant, and I smiled back, loving the merriness in his eyes and the way I felt so comfortable with him. His smile was dangerous, threatening to steal my heart. Then again, it was time to quit avoiding the message my own heart had been signaling to me, for quite some time now.

That theft had already taken place.

Time alone with Daniel was all too rare, and I decided right then and there that I would not give it up even to include Casey.

Breakfast burritos for two, and not three, it was.

"Your mom doesn't know where your dad lives?"

It was a perfect Saturday morning, warm with a slight breeze. Our bench was under a shady tree, and though it wasn't exactly secluded we had plenty of privacy since hardly anyone was at the park.

I swallowed a bite of my egg and sausage burrito. Daniel had practically inhaled three of them, while I had barely touched mine since I was doing most of the talking. "All she knows is that after his senior year, Josh went off to college and his father- my grandfather- accepted a job transfer to another state. Mom learned that information from a friend. She and I didn't move back here until I was five though, and by that time most of her former friends were busy with their own families or careers or had moved away.

"Actually, it's a relief to know that Josh didn't know about me. I don't mean that I'm glad Mom handled things the way she did, it's just that my dad didn't *abandon* me. If he had known Mom was pregnant and just ignored her or refused to help, that would have been awful. But he didn't know. So, in a way, he's kind of innocent. He wasn't given the *chance* to be responsible."

Daniel mulled this over. "I see your point, though maybe the word innocent isn't the best word. After all, he cheated on your mom. He gave her a fairly good reason not to trust him."

When I didn't respond, he gave me a sideways look. "You

know Reese, maybe you're being a bit hard on your mom. Imagine being in her situation right now, and the person you thought was your entire world let you down. Maybe you would have chosen a different path than your mom did, that's true, but it seems to me like she's been a good mother."

He reached for my hand and squeezed it. "She raised a strong, smart, independent daughter who cares about other people and tends to see the best in them, even if they don't deserve it. Maybe she made a mistake, a big one, but we all do."

I took in his words, appreciating his kindness and considering the truth of what he said. If I had been in Mom's predicament, would I have handled things differently? It was hard to say. Her story was not mine, and it's easy to judge when you haven't experienced another person's problems, or their options.

I squeezed his hand back, and we sat there for another minute until Daniel finally spoke.

"We need some frivolity," he said very seriously. "And I've been waiting for just this moment. Reese, truth or dare?"

I could not switch moods that easily, and I looked over at him, startled. "What?"

"You heard me. I distinctly remember having this game explained to me by you and Casey. It's a way for friends to get to know each other better, correct? So, pick one."

"Not so fast, Dixon," I responded, sitting up a bit straighter and pulling my hand away. "I've been spilling my guts to you all morning, so you have to be the one who starts telling me your deep dark secrets."

His eyes sparkled. "Fair enough. I pick dare."

I rolled my eyes. "Of course you do, that's who you are. You are a totally dare kind of person."

"Why, thank you. C'mon, gimme a dare. I've got this."

Hmmm. So, so many possibilities, but my mind rapidly

zeroed in on only one. Daniel knew an awful lot about me and my family now, and there didn't seem to be much I couldn't tell him...

I blurted it out before I could overthink.

"I dare you to explain to me exactly why you don't want to be my boyfriend."

CHAPTER 16

"Sneaky. A truth wrapped up in a dare. Well played, legend."
Daniel looked at me admiringly, not seeming at all bothered by
my question.

I waited, now on full alert for his answer. "Well?"

Daniel stood up and stretched. "Man, that bench is hard.
Let's walk around."

I stood up, gathering my trash and throwing it away, since
Daniel had already disposed of his. When he held out his hand
again, though, I shook my head. "Nope, friends don't usually
hold hands unless they're five years old, so none of that
anymore. I'm serious. We're in this weird friend zone that's not
quite staying in the boundaries, and I need boundaries. We
walk, you talk." I started briskly down the concrete sidewalk
that meandered through the park, not waiting for him to
follow.

He caught up with me easily. "It's more fun when we hold
hands," he said plaintively, but I ignored him, and he heaved
this big dramatic sigh. "Okay, you're right. You deserve to know
what I'm thinking. I'm always going to be completely honest
with you, Reese. Do you believe that?"

86

I didn't hesitate. "I do. Keep talking."

"Thank you. I warn you, this may be a long walk, because this is a long story. So. Remember last fall when I wanted to ask you to the Homecoming dance? I waited too late, so I changed my game plan and decided instead to ask you to Prom. I'm not much on dating etiquette and promposals and all that stuff, so I asked Casey to coach me on all things Reese."

I nodded. "Casey told me about that. She found out my favorite things and made you a list, in exchange for your help on some of her school projects."

"Exactly, and she drives a hard bargain, but she was useful. The best thing Casey gave me, though, was this sheet of paper that had Bible verses on it, all about what real love means."

"She gave me those verses too," I admitted. "In fact, my mom and I were just talking about that very thing the other day."

"'Love is patient, love is kind. It does not envy, it does not boast'- I've been told I need to work on that – 'it is not proud. It does not dishonor others, it is not self-seeking, it is not easily angered, it keeps no record of wrongs. Love does not delight in evil but rejoices with the truth. It always protects, always trusts, always hopes, always perseveres.' I memorized it, Reese.

"At the time, it was awkward because as I told Casey, I only wanted to ask you to prom and not to marry me or anything crazy like that. Love wasn't exactly on my mind. But then I got to know you better."

He paused, and my heart started beating faster. "And?"

"And..." He hesitated. "This is the part where you might run away screaming, okay?"

I stopped in my tracks. "Good thing I have on my tennis shoes. Just tell me, Daniel.

He stopped too, turning to face me. There no one around because I hurriedly checked.

"In sports, we're coached to play the long game," he said, looking at me intently. "To plan ahead, to skip quick fixes in favor of strategies that build for the future. As I spent more time with you, I realized that this is what I want, Reese. I don't care too much about one dance, or dating for a few weeks, or whatever. I want a real relationship with someone I care about. A future. I want that with you.

"I realize you may not feel the same way, so there's absolutely no pressure. I mean that. You don't have to feel like you're breaking my heart or anything because who knows? We're young and maybe my own feelings will change, though I don't think so."

I tried to absorb his words, though my mind was stuck on the *I want that with you* part. In contrast, my heart was soaring.

"Well, you're not running away," Daniel observed, but he didn't smile. "Look, Reese, all that I said comes down to this- I've decided to honor God in this way. I want to practice what those verses say about love, with you. To play the long game, become best friends and *show* you love, and not just say it or only express it physically. I want to build the kind of relationship that will last longer than high school. Way longer."

"With me," I repeated, searching his face for any sign that he might be regretting those words.

He swallowed, and I saw the Daniel that most of Rayburn High would never see, vulnerable and dead serious. "With you."

The vow I had made came instantly to mind. *No more high school boyfriends.* It was a fair enough resolution, but there was pain behind that vow. I had put up a wall to shut out risks, to protect my heart, leaving no entrances or exits. Could a decision built on fear really be a good one?

My thoughts cleared. I could see another path, one that had been there all along. It seemed risky too, but there would be possibilities, instead of a dead end.

Taking a step closer to Daniel, my heartbeat was steady, my voice calm. "Daniel, I'm sorry, but I don't think we can remain friends." He looked startled, and then a bit panicked. Closing the space between us, I watched his expression turn to confusion.

"Not *just* friends," I said softly. "But maybe best friends, like you said, with a future." I took his hand, stood on my tiptoes, and did what I had wanted to do for a long time now.

I kissed him tenderly on his cheek, feeling the scratchiness where he hadn't shaved that morning, and wrapped my arms around him. He held me close, his chin resting on my head, and we stayed that way for a long time, making no other promises than a silent one, to try to love each other the way love was meant to be. I felt safe.

"Reese?"

I snuggled closer into our hug. "Yes?"

"Truth or dare?"

Incredulous, I pulled away from him. Why would Daniel break this perfect moment? When I saw his face, though, beaming with pure joy, I couldn't stop my grin and then I started chuckling. He joined in and we clung to each other, laughing once again until we had tears in our eyes.

I hoped we would always be this way, able to laugh together, and for the first time in way too long, I silently opted for the dare choice. I dared to hope.

Thank you.

This time, I knew who I was thanking. I felt him, his words calling me to a love richer and deeper than what I could understand right now. This love wasn't about me and Daniel, though.

This hope, this love, was about me and God.

CHAPTER 17

"Mom?" It wasn't that late, and I found Mom sitting in the office, working on her laptop.

"Come in, baby. How was Jackson's graduation party?" She stopped typing and gave me her full attention, obviously relieved that I was speaking to her again.

"Fun. Can we talk?"

Mom cocked her head at me, a wry smile on her face. "Now, what do you think? I will never, ever turn down the chance to talk to my girl."

I walked over and stood behind her chair, wrapping my arms around her in a loose bear hug. "I'm sorry," I whispered. "Sorry I shut you out. I'm sorry I judged you, when I don't know what I would have done myself if I had been in your same situation."

Mom wrapped her own arms around mine, as she sat in the chair. "You have nothing to apologize for, Reese. But will you forgive *me*?"

"Done. I'll probably still get mad about it, but then I'll just have to forgive you again."

"I think that's how it goes," she agreed. "Thank you, Reesie. We'll work through this. Have you decided if you want to find your father?"

"No, I need time to think about it for a while. I have something else to tell you, though." I wasn't ready to talk to her about Daniel and the new "friends-with-a-future" conversation we had this morning. That was too new, too personal. This topic was personal, too, but Mom of all people would understand. "Can we go upstairs and talk?"

"Will we need ice cream?" she teased. "Or chocolate?"

"It can only help," I agreed, releasing her from my hug. "I didn't eat that much at the party."

We gathered some cheese and crackers instead, and went upstairs, settling this time on the little loveseat in Mom's bedroom. Grandma had probably already gone to bed, but it was still nice to know we wouldn't be interrupted.

"So, what's going on?"

I dove right in. "I've made up my mind about God. I believe he really is out there. And not just that, but I believe that he's *here*. Here with me, and you.

"I've been talking to him lately, just simple stuff like saying thank you, but you know all the things I've heard at the youth group meetings? It makes more sense now. During all this madness with Ethan, my friends have been here for me. Daniel supports me. God is here, through them, helping me."

I finally looked at Mom, and saw that her eyes were "leaking," as she liked to call it. "You don't need to cry, Mom," I teased her, though I was tearing up a little bit, too.

Mom swiped at her eyes. "It's just that I've been thinking the same thing, Reese. I've been reading in the Bible that Karen gave me, and I can see God everywhere now. Even years ago, when life as I knew it was over, he was there, giving me the hope to continue my pregnancy and raise you myself, and all the steps after that. My problems didn't go away, but he sent encouragement and help from others when I needed it. Even when I didn't pay attention, he never gave up on me."

"That's just it, Mom. That verse keeps popping up, the one you mentioned a few days ago. You know, the one that talks about how love never gives up? How it protects and hopes, and all that? I want to know the God who wrote that. The one who loves me like that." I didn't tell her that Daniel had quoted that same verse to me this morning.

"I do, too, Reese. I want to know him and follow him. From what I understand, it takes faith."

My heart started beating faster. "Then let's do it. Right now."

"Now?" Mom looked surprised. "Don't we need to be in church or something?"

"Nope. It's a decision we can make anywhere. I know that from the youth meetings." Excited, I felt the same hope rising that I had recognized earlier. "At the end of every single meeting, the youth pastor prays this prayer with those who want to say it, and it's short. I may not get all the words exactly right, but I don't think it matters since we're just having a conversation with God. Are you in?"

Mom beamed at me and reached over to grasp my hand tightly. "I'm in. You go first."

I bowed my head and closed my eyes. I didn't think I had to, but it seemed respectful. "Jesus, I believe that you are the son of God. I believe that you died for my sins because you love me, and that you rose again and are alive today. Forgive me for all my sins." I gave up on not crying at this point, and my next words were a whisper. "Forgive me for all the ways I've messed up and hurt other people, and for all the selfish decisions I've made. I want to know you and follow your ways."

I had a lot more to say, but Mom needed her turn, and I could talk to God later, I knew. "Okay, Mom, you're up."

She chuckled through her own tears and said pretty much the same short prayer, in her own words. When she was done, we sat quietly, processing.

"We did it, Reese," Mom finally said, her voice sounding a little awe-struck. "We belong to Jesus now."

I grinned, leaning back on the loveseat. "And we did it together, Mom. That's pretty cool."

"So. what's next? Is there something we're supposed to do next?"

I considered this, a little stumped, but then for some reason Daniel's grinning face came to mind and I smiled.

"I think we celebrate, Mom. Let's move on to some ice cream and enjoy the moment!"

We did that, choosing to sit at the kitchen table this time to eat our double dutch chocolate. "Maybe we should go to church tomorrow," I suggested.

"Maybe," Mom agreed, "but I'm sure Grandma's planning a big brunch like she always does, and I would hate for her to feel like we don't value that. It means a lot to her." We discussed it and decided we would tell Grandma about the decisions we had made over brunch tomorrow, sticking to our usual schedule, and then figure things out from there.

"Did Grandma and Grandpa ever take you to church when you were growing up?" I never knew my grandpa since he had died before I was born. I did know that he had left Grandma for another woman years before that. It had always been just another reason for the Owens women to not trust men.

"Actually, yes, when I was pretty small." Mom's brow creased. "I never told you this part, Reese, but there's a reason we stopped going to church, after my father left Grandma, that I didn't know about for years." She paused.

"This is a rather heavy subject, since you and I are brand new Christians, but we just have to face it head on. Your Aunt Rachel told me that the other woman Dad left Mother for was a member of our church. They met there, and she was married as well. It was a huge scandal.

"Like I said, I didn't know that part until I was thirteen, when my father passed away. It's a big reason why I wouldn't give God a chance for so long, and why I believed Christians were hypocrites."

Her eyes were sad. "It's also a reason why Grandma didn't argue with me too much when I wanted to go live with Rachel my senior year, and not tell Josh about the pregnancy. Grandma knew what it was like to feel betrayed. Even if she didn't agree with me, she let me decide. She understood."

I swirled the last of my melted ice cream with a spoon. My heart ached for Grandma, and for Mom. Would every decision we made, good or bad, always impact those we loved?

"And she started Your Perfect Day after that. A wedding business. So ironic!"

Mom nodded, seeming lost in her own thoughts.

I sat up straight, suddenly remembering something else Daniel had asked me before we parted ways this morning.

"Mom, I totally forgot! Daniel's Uncle Danny would like to get in touch with you, and he asked about the best way to do that. I didn't give him any contact info, don't worry," I added quickly when Mom looked alarmed. "I'm only the messenger."

She relaxed, then started gathering our spoons and bowls. "I'll think about that and get back to you," she said rather formally, and I suppressed a grin. I had just used that line on Ethan.

Ethan! I almost groaned. I did need to talk with him. But not tonight, I told myself, as I hugged Mom and headed back upstairs. I wasn't getting in touch with anyone tonight, except Jesus. Not even Daniel.

Jesus and I had a *whole* bunch to talk about.

CHAPTER 18

Casey and I had a whole bunch to talk about, too, and I decided I might as well include Mia and Abby in my big information download since they were also my close friends. My group text message on Sunday morning was mysterious and short:

> Life changing news! My house, 3 pm, be there! Sorry for the short notice.

Grinning, I hit send, then headed downstairs in my pajamas, following the aroma of cinnamon and coffee. "Cinnamon rolls?" I asked hopefully as I entered the kitchen.

"With fresh fruit, to keep things healthier," Grandma responded cheerfully. "I cheated and used some frozen dough, however."

"We won't tell anyone," Mom said from where she sat at the table, already holding her cup of coffee. "Next week, though, you take a break and Reese and I will treat *you*, since school will be out this week. Maybe we can make some adjustments. We'll talk about that later," she added, giving me a meaningful look.

I winked at her and loaded up my plate. "Mmmm,

cantaloupe is my favorite. I think today will be my perfect day, Grandma, thanks to this breakfast."

She sniffed as she sat down at the table. "It takes more than just food to coordinate a perfect day."

"We had a tough gig yesterday while you were at the graduation ceremony," Mom explained. "The minister mixed up the times, wasn't answering his phone and finally strolled in thirty minutes late to the wedding! Then at the reception, the music the bride chose was wildly inappropriate and made a lot of guests uncomfortable."

"Don't forget the children," Grandma said grimly, and I almost spit out my orange juice.

"Let me guess," I said before Mom could continue. "Children were invited and got hyped up on sugar? Five pieces of wedding cake each?"

"Their parents weren't watching them," Mom sighed.

"Savages," Grandma muttered.

I giggled. "So, the bride's perfect day turned out to be just an okay day, huh?"

"The bride was a sweetheart, very easygoing even though her choice in wedding music was alarming," Mom allowed.

"Well," I said, seeing this as a good opening, "Mom and I had a very good day yesterday, Grandma."

She swallowed a piece of her fruit and looked at Mom and I quizzically. "Since you two didn't seem to spend any time together yesterday, I'm anxious to know the details."

Mom nodded at me, and I opened my mouth to answer Grandma when I realized that as far as I knew, Grandma still didn't know that Mom had spilled the beans about my father to me, just last week. We had not included her in any of our private conversations for the last several days. Should I talk about that now, too?

Noticing my hesitation, Mom must have thought I was

nervous because she took over. She told Grandma how she and I had made the decision to pray last night and put our trust in Jesus. Grandma listened intently, not saying anything after Mom had finished, and we waited, a little awkwardly. Grandma was never at a loss for words.

Finally, Grandma picked up her napkin, dabbed at her mouth, and then cleared her throat. "I'm happy for each of you," she said. "It seems that you both put a lot of thought into this. Now, I'll just clear up these dishes."

I looked at Mom and she gave a little shrug. "No, Mother, Reese and I will handle that. You go sit down and rest now. I'm sure glad we don't have an event this afternoon."

Without another word, Grandma got up and left the room, leaving me feeling a bit disappointed. I understood her reaction, though. Even a week ago, I'm not sure how I would have responded to someone telling me they had decided to trust in a God I wasn't convinced even existed. Grandma *had* believed in God, though, at least years ago. Didn't she?

I pondered this while Mom and I quietly loaded the dishwasher and stored the leftover cinnamon rolls.

My girls, however, were not nearly as restrained.

"There is so much to tell you," I moaned. We were in my bedroom, sitting cross legged on my bed in a little circle. "I'm not sure where to even start."

"*Start at the very beginning, a very good place to start,*" Mia sang in her sweet voice, and I recognized the famous tune from The Sound of Music. Mia took part in a school musical earlier this spring and was always humming show tunes now at random moments.

"Okay, but that means going back a long time ago," I warned them. Starting in, I told them about Mom's story when she was seventeen. I went on with the information I had learned about my father, including the fact that Daniel's uncle had known Mom in high school.

"Which means he can probably guess who your dad is," Abby said astutely.

"True. But *he's* not my dad, which would have been horrible. Not because Uncle Danny is a bad person or anything, but..." I hesitated.

"If Daniel's uncle was your dad, then you and Daniel would be cousins. Related. That would be tragic." Casey shuddered.

"Because Daniel is crazy about you, and not in a cousinly way," Mia agreed. "Everybody knows that!"

"About that." I grinned, and Casey shrieked.

"About *that*? You and Daniel? Finally?"

"The sparks were sure flying at bowling the other night. I was about ready to call the fire department," Abby teased.

"Quit interrupting and let her finish," Mia begged. "What happened? When? Spill it!"

I told them briefly about my conversation yesterday morning with Daniel, and our new and improved friend status. When I finished, instead of the exuberance I expected, my friends were strangely quiet.

"You mean to tell me that Daniel memorized those Bible verses I gave him?" Casey looked astonished. "That boy actually took them to heart?"

"And now *you're* in his heart," Mia breathed. "This is honestly the most romantic thing I have ever heard in my life, Reese."

"But that's not all," I said grandly. "I've saved the very best part for last."

"What on earth is better than that? I'm about to have a heart attack! Tell us," Abby begged. "Quick!"

"This is better." I told them about my decision, and Mom's,

to follow Jesus, and the things that led us to that. "You each had a part in this, you know. Being in youth group with me and never making me feel uncomfortable there, and standing by me when Ethan made that post. And of course, the verses you gave to both me and Daniel," I added, nodding at Casey.

"You're right, Reese, this really is the best news of all," Mia agreed. "Group hug!"

"It's more like a group *cry*," Abby joked as we all leaned in for the hug, rather awkwardly. She was right since we all had happy tears in our eyes.

"And now, ice cream," I told them. "It's an Owens thing."

"Long live the Owens women," Casey said, still appearing a bit overwhelmed. "May God bless them with lots of ice cream, forever and ever, amen."

And lots of good friends," I added as we each got off the bed, stretched, and headed downstairs.

CHAPTER 19

This Thursday night, one of the Owens women was in a tizzy, as nervous as a squirrel in traffic, because Daniel and his Uncle Danny were coming to dinner.

"Remind me why we invited them again?" Mom asked, sounding irritated, but I knew it was just a cover for her anxiety.

"We invited Danny here because you refused to go alone on a date with him when he contacted you the other day, remember?" I was stretched out on her bed, watching Mom examine herself in the full-length mirror mounted on her closet door.

"Lies," Mom muttered. "Does this outfit seem appropriate? And Danny did not ask me out on a date."

"Oh, I would say that 'Ruby, could we catch up over dinner?' sounds like a date. And if it's *not* a date, why worry about your outfit?"

"Please remove yourself from this room, young lady. No, don't go, I need support. I'm a nervous wreck! Why am I so nervous?" I think Mom started out talking to me, but now it sounded like she was questioning her inner therapist.

"Mommm!" I sighed and rolled off her bed, taking time to

stretch, and headed for the bedroom door. "I need to go freshen up for my own non-date. Everything will be fine."

I believed that, but then any time I got to spend with Daniel seemed to make my world spin more smoothly, even with so many things still unresolved. I hadn't contacted Ethan yet, and the decision of whether to find my father was still on the backburner of my mind.

But so many things were going great, I reminded myself as I entered my own bedroom. School had been out for over a week, and I was now an official wedding planner intern, with two gigs coming up this weekend. Daniel had started his own job as a summer camp counselor at the local YMCA and appeared to be a natural working with the kids. Grandma was now fully updated about all the dad developments, and she and Mom both seemed pleased, if cautious, about my "friends with a future" status with Daniel. Best of all, though, I had a sense of peace, a confidence that everything would work out, even the hard stuff, under God's watch.

My phone dinged.

Leaving. Be there in a few.

I smiled at Daniel's text, brushed my hair a bit, and decided to go downstairs and assemble the salad. Mom had put a beef casserole in the oven earlier, and I could already smell the savory aroma wafting through the house. Laying my brush down, I stopped to check my phone when it dinged again, with another message.

Tonight? Can I come over and talk to you?

Ethan again. Ever since I had made it clear that I would contact him when I was ready, I hadn't heard anything at all from him. Maybe I should have felt annoyed with this text, but instead I felt guilty. What if he truly wanted to apologize and make things right? Shouldn't I give him the chance to do that? Who was I to withhold forgiveness, when I had been forgiven of so much, myself?

Later, I promised myself. *I'll text him tomorrow.* I skipped downstairs, not only ready for Daniel's company, but also curious about how Mom's reunion would go with this casual friend from her past. The one who also knew my father, and last but not least-

-the man who once had a huge crush on her.

Uncle Danny had been nice-looking when I met him the first time in Daniel's kitchen, wearing his police uniform, but in his jeans and button-down shirt? He was rather swoony, for a thirty-four-year-old. Oddly, I felt my guard go up as I re-introduced him to his old friend, my mom. He must have noticed the *don't mess with my mother* warning in my eyes, because his own gaze met mine with understanding. Giving me a deferential nod, he greeted Mom in a friendly, but impersonal way.

Between Grandma's impeccable social skills and Daniel's funny stories about the kids at summer camp, everyone finally relaxed, and we were all laughing as we finished our meal.

"Shall we have dessert on the patio?" Grandma suggested. "It's a pleasant evening, and not too humid yet." We all agreed, getting up to assemble our bowls of strawberry shortcake in the kitchen, and carrying them outside. We all sat around the patio table.

"This is my all-time favorite dessert," Danny proclaimed. "How could y'all have known that?"

"We didn't, but I'm glad you like it. Mother baked the

shortcake from scratch." Mom hesitated, glanced at me, and appeared to make a decision. "Danny, I want to ask you a rather serious question, if you don't mind. Reese has told Daniel about her father situation, so I'm assuming you also know why I left Bonham High my senior year?"

We all looked at Danny, who kept his attention fixed on Mom. "No, Ruby, Daniel hasn't told me anything about your story. He wouldn't do that unless he had your permission, or Reese's." He hesitated. "However, since you have a seventeen-year-old daughter, I'm assuming you were, uh, in the family way?"

For the first time, he seemed uncomfortable and shifted in his chair, but Mom just smiled. "The official word is 'pregnant' Danny. That is correct. The first time Reese mentioned your name, and I realized you were Daniel's uncle, I knew that you might know who her father is. The thing is, *he* doesn't know about *Reese*."

Comprehension dawned on Danny's face, and he scooted forward a bit in his chair. Looking at me, he sent a silent question which I somehow understood.

"I know all the details, Officer. I even found his location on an internet search, though he doesn't seem to have any social media accounts except for a business one. His picture on that account looks like an older version of his high school pic, though. Mom is also sure it's him because it lists our town as one where he lived before, and she recognized the names of his sister and parents, which also show up."

"Please, call me Danny. And just to verify, you're talking about Josh Lockwood?"

"He's the one," Mom said, her voice dry. "I'm glad you didn't have to think too hard about who the father was. He was my only boyfriend in high school."

"I remember that. I remember watching you and him

together and wishing..." Danny looked at Mom steadily. "You were too good for him, Ruby."

Grandma cleared her throat, and though Mom didn't smile she gave Danny a long, measuring look.

"That is to say, I mean, Josh was smart and could be a good guy," he backtracked, frowning. He looked again at me. "He has a wonderful daughter, so he couldn't be terrible. Reese, I didn't mean... what I do know is that I should just keep my mouth shut." He did just that finally, looking embarrassed and apologetic. "I'm sorry."

"Don't be." Grandma finally spoke up. "That two-timin' rattlesnake cheated on my daughter!"

I rolled my eyes and Daniel and his uncle looked like they wished they were a million miles away, eyeing each other uneasily.

"More shortcake?" Grandma added calmly, and Mom started chuckling. Taking her cue, Daniel smiled, too, and finally his uncle sighed, straightening his shoulders.

"I'll take another piece, ma'am, but not before I say this- Josh was just a boy, Ruby. That doesn't excuse him one bit, but you? You rose to the occasion and were strong, obviously, in a way that he could not be at the time. I always saw that strength in you, even as a boy myself. I just want you to know that. I saw that. And it doesn't surprise me to see you here today, making a beautiful life for you and your daughter."

I held my breath, waiting for Mom's response. It was a sweet thing for Danny to tell her, and I hoped she would receive it. Stealing a glance at her, I figured that she did, since she was blushing like a thirteen-year-old girl who had just been told by her crush that she was pretty. Grabbing Daniel's hand, I pulled him to his feet. "We'll bring the shortcake supplies out here so we can finish our conversation, okay? You come help us, Grandma."

Following my lead, Grandma stood up primly, smoothing her shirt, and met up with Daniel and me in the kitchen.

"Are you scheming, young lady?" she asked tartly, as she got the whipped cream out of the refrigerator.

"I've decided to trust him. They need some time alone," I whispered to her, and she just shook her head, the beginning of a smile on her face.

"Did you see the look on Uncle Danny's face there at the end?" Daniel asked both of us, a bit in awe. "He looked...what's the right word?"

Grandma patted his shoulder as she handed him the bowl of strawberries. "Your uncle looked at Ruby the way you look at my granddaughter, young man. I believe the appropriate word is 'smitten'."

"Smitten!" Daniel nodded and grinned at me. "That sums it up, Mrs. Owens. Smitten sums it up nicely."

This time it was my turn to blush, at the tender look in his eyes, and I couldn't look away.

CHAPTER 20

I slept in the next morning, knowing that this afternoon and tomorrow would be jam-packed, with two weddings on Saturday and two appointments later today.

Taking a leisurely shower, I spent extra time fixing my hair and make-up, hoping for a professional and put-together look that didn't scream "high school" Our first meeting today was with a newly engaged bride and her mother who were considering using Grandma's services, and I was attending as her assistant.

My phone was still on the charger, so it was almost eleven o'clock by the time I checked for new messages. When I finally did, however, I saw another text from Ethan.

I know about your father.

Um, what?

Confused, I stared at the message again and started to rub my eyes until I remembered I didn't want to smudge my mascara. Instead, I inhaled, closed my eyes briefly to hopefully clear my vision, and read the message again.

Yep. Same words. How on earth would Ethan know anything about my father?

Carefully laying the phone down on the bedside table, I forced myself to sit on the edge of my bed and think, taking another deep breath. My thoughts were scrambling with possible answers to my question. I had never mentioned a single thing to Ethan about my mother or any of my family while we were hanging out, and he never took any interest anyway. The only people besides Mom and Grandma who knew about my recent dad discoveries were my closest friends, who I could count on just one hand. Plus, Daniel's uncle, of course.

Doubts started creeping in. Had one of my friends let my secrets slip out? Maybe Abby had told her mother, who told another friend - these things happened. Perhaps Casey had mentioned it to her boyfriend? Or did Daniel...?

I ruled that thought out immediately. Daniel would never break my confidence, especially with Ethan, of that I was sure. Casey wouldn't either, nor any of my friends, and I just couldn't see Uncle Danny sharing my confidential information with anyone at all. I chose to have faith in my friends, but it left me frustrated. Ethan knew *something*, and I knew from experience that he was no mind-reader.

The phone dinged again, and this time when I read Ethan's message, my confusion turned to shock.

Meet me in your backyard now.

Ethan was in my *backyard*?

Frustration built as I slipped on some shoes. I was already wearing the blouse and skirt I had chosen for the bride's meeting at one o'clock, and I didn't want to get sweaty by staying out in the humid weather for too long. How dare Ethan make demands on me? Showing up unannounced and uninvited in my backyard? I would march downstairs right now and grab Mom or Grandma, and we would settle things with Ethan in a decisive and proper way, once and for all.

I was on the top step when the next message came.

> You said you would talk to me. Please. Just a few minutes.

My steps slowed, halfway down the staircase. I did tell Ethan I would contact him, and that had been weeks ago. I did believe that he was a decent guy at heart- hadn't I told my counselor that, and Mom and Grandma? I had been thoughtless, dismissing his request to talk to me because so many other things were on my mind. Such as, my father.

Who he seemed to know about.

Grandma appeared from our office, holding her cell phone. "Reese? We leave in an hour and a half, so we'll fix some lunch as soon as I make this call. Your mother left to run a few errands." Giving me a little wave, she disappeared again inside the office.

Yay. That ruled out any immediate support from the other Owens women, and I hesitated there on the steps, forming a quick, silent prayer. *Help me with this conversation, please.* Hurrying down the rest of the stairs, I crossed over into the kitchen, opened the back door and stepped outside onto the patio.

And there was Ethan, slumped casually in the same chair that Daniel had sat in just last night, wearing a Rayburn High ball cap.

"Reese." His voice was low and warm, and he smiled at me, looking as if I should be pleased to see him, as if I had invited him here.

I shook my head, amazed. "Why are you in my backyard, Ethan? You just came in through our gate without permission?"

"Like a friend does."

"More like a stalker," I retorted, and then something finally clicked. "You were here last night, weren't you? You sneaked in through the gate and listened to the conversation my family and I were having with our guests. Our *private* conversation." I struggled to stay calm, though anger was building in my gut.

Ethan shrugged, still smiling. "I texted you last night, and since you never answered I decided to just come over. I heard voices in the backyard and thought you might be outside. I never intended to eavesdrop."

I crossed my arms, cocking my head. "Actually, you did intend to eavesdrop. At any point you could have left the yard, or walked over to the patio to let us know you were there. And then, you send me a creepy message saying that you know about my father? This is so wrong, Ethan."

He stood up and took a step toward me. "It was an accident, Reese. You should have answered my text or contacted me long before now. Then this would never have happened."

I must have looked murderous because he hastily went on. "I can take you to your father, Reese. I know where he is. In fact, I talked"-

"Leave. My. Father. Out of this." I spoke through gritted teeth. "You have to leave right now, Ethan. I need to process everything you just said and try to make sense of who you are. I feel like I don't even *know* you. And you've never even apologized for that awful post you made." Standing here with Ethan in front of me, the memory of that night, with its guilt, embarrassment, and shame, came back in full force.

Something shifted in Ethan's expression and though he still smiled, it was strained. "That was a mistake. You made me angry, and I overreacted. If you had only just talked things through with me, that post would never have happened."

So, it was all my fault? Ethan's ability to turn things around, to make me responsible for his own poor choices, left me stunned. I remembered my school counselor's words from our short visit a few weeks ago: *You are not responsible for Ethan's behavior in any way.*

Ethan took another step toward me, his expression now serious, regretful. "It's a shame, Reese. You and me, we're a perfect couple. For sure we're better than you and Dixon." His lip curled, and the awful name he then called Daniel made my eyes widen.

I held my ground, not backing away, but then wondered if I should. Would Ethan physically hurt me? I didn't think so, but then again, I hadn't realized he was capable of becoming the insensitive intruder he clearly was right now. Remembering my phone was in my skirt pocket, I casually, slowly moved my hand there. Maybe I could grab it and somehow call for help? Would Ethan try to stop me?

He took another step forward, his face now only inches away from mine, and I involuntarily took a step back. I felt chilled now, clammy, though it was probably high noon and already a sweltering day.

"Don't be upset, Reese," Ethan said softly, intimately. "Let's talk it out."

Get by the kitchen window. The thought came instantly. Yes, Grandma would be done with her phone call soon. She would be making lunch in the kitchen and would see us through the window. I didn't want to endanger her, but I could signal her, or just scream. That might be a better plan than fumbling with the phone.

I stood up straight, determined to not cower in front of Ethan. "Yes, we'll talk," I answered, keeping my voice steady. "Let's just pull a couple of chairs over here, more in the shade." I walked over to the patio table and started moving a chair over by the kitchen window, dragging the legs on the concrete to make as much noise as possible. I noticed movement in the kitchen and immediately gained some confidence.

"Here, I'll get that," Ethan offered as I reached for a second chair. He seemed pleased. "We'll take our time, though I have to be at work at two."

You honestly assume that I want to spend even one more minute with you? Ethan had always been self-centered, but his behavior now was way, way over the top. Instead of voicing my inner thoughts, however, I forced a smile, then spoke almost in a shout, focusing on the kitchen window intently.

"Sure, Ethan! Let's talk about how you sneaked into our backyard last night!"

Grandma's startled face appeared at the kitchen window, and I mouthed "help me" to her before turning back to face Ethan, now seated in one of the chairs. His eyes narrowed, then darted to the kitchen window, recognizing that perhaps we were being observed.

He didn't move, however, even when Grandma opened the back door. "Reese?" She practically ran onto the patio, wielding a frying pan. "Ethan? What in tarnation are you doing here in my yard?"

Ethan stood, looking warily at Grandma, but his voice was respectful. "Hello, Mrs. Owens, nice to see you again. I was just-"

"GET. OUT." Grandma was seething, and she took a menacing step towards Ethan, lifting the frying pan. I hurriedly grabbed my phone and called 911.

"He didn't touch me, Grandma," I intervened somewhat reluctantly, after I punched in the numbers. My elegant grandmother rarely used the word "tarnation" anymore unless she was extremely upset, and I was touched by her protective instincts.

The 911 operator answered and began asking me questions, and I put the phone on speaker mode.

Ethan was indignant. "What are you doing?"

Ignoring him, I continued answering the questions being asked of me, while Ethan sputtered, apparently aghast. Grandma positioned herself between me and him, but before I even finished the call, Ethan strode angrily out of the yard, leaving the same way he had entered. This time, however, he slammed the gate so hard that it shook.

CHAPTER 21

Casey's eyes were as round as saucers. "What happened next?"

"Well," I drawled. "Grandma and I ate lunch, and then we went to our appointment."

"AAAGGHH," Casey moaned, like I knew she would. "You know what I mean! Did the police come? Did they find Ethan? What happens now?"

"I'm not sure," I admitted. "Ethan could be charged with trespassing, but he didn't damage anything, and he did leave after Grandma told him to go, even though he didn't do it right away. I think the police went to find him after they left our house, and they probably contacted his parents. It's just a mess. *He's* a mess."

We were sitting at my kitchen table, along with Daniel and Ben, this Friday night. Daniel had already heard all the details, but he listened just as intently now as he had earlier, when he came over right after work.

Ducking my head, I stared down at the placemat in front of me. "I do worry, though, that I overreacted. Ethan didn't actually threaten or hurt me. Calling 911 seemed like a good idea at the time, but it was probably unnecessary." When nobody said anything, I peeked up at Casey, sitting across from me. Did she agree?

She was staring at me, shocked, and Daniel was the first to speak, so I swiveled my head to look at him, sitting beside me.

His blue eyes were steely, his expression fierce. "Reese, if it was Casey telling this story, if this had happened to her, would you tell her she overreacted?"

"Of course not," I admitted, relaxing my shoulders a bit. I hadn't thought of it that way. But Daniel wasn't finished.

"You felt nervous for a good reason, enough to do something about it by figuring out how to get your grandmother's attention. Ethan didn't leave when *you* told him to. He twisted everything around to make that social media post seem like it was all your fault." Daniel shook his head slowly, his eyes holding mine, pleading with me to accept his words. "He tried to play the victim and plant these ideas in your head that you are the one mistreating *him*. That's, that's..."

"Sick!" Casey finished for him, sitting back in her chair and crossing her arms, eyes blazing. "Manipulative. Narcissistic."

"And don't forget," Ben chimed in, "that he trespassed in your yard not just once, but twice, and learned personal information he had no business knowing. He then used that information to get you to meet him outside."

"Well, when you put it that way..." I paused. "That's all true. Speaking of the personal information, keep in mind that Ethan said he knew where my father is." I frowned, trying to remember if he had revealed anything more. Some small detail tugged at my brain, just out of reach. "I interrupted him because I was so angry. Maybe I'll remember if he said anything else of importance, a little later. But right now, y'all, I need a change of subject. I don't want to waste one more brain cell on Ethan. Is anyone hungry? Should we order in pizza?"

"One last thing." Daniel's voice was low, and he scooted his chair closer to mine, wrapping one arm around my shoulders and tugging me close to him. "Always trust your instincts, okay?"

"Unless your instincts tell you to jump out of an airplane with no parachute," Casey pointed out logically.

Daniel ignored her and kissed the top of my head. "And use good sense. Which you did."

"And pray. I did that first," I whispered. Daniel pulled me a tad closer, and using my best instincts and good sense, I allowed him to do only that and no more.

"Ahem." Ben coughed dramatically, even as he and Casey grinned at each other. "My instincts are telling me that yes, we need pizza as soon as possible."

"And we can stream an alien movie," Casey added cheerfully. "That's just good sense."

In the end, we decided to go out for pizza instead, though we didn't stay out too late since I needed to rest up for work the next day. I never did recall that stray memory, about the other thing Ethan was trying to say when I interrupted him.

As it turned out, I didn't need to work on remembering it, because the subject of his unfinished sentence managed to find its way to me. More accurately-

-*he* found his way to me.

CHAPTER 22

After a hectic Saturday, Mom and I went to church on Sunday morning and sat with Casey's family. Her oldest stepbrother was now home from college for the summer, and with her mom, stepdad, three stepbrothers, little sister, and Ben, that made ten of us, taking up most of an entire row. I liked the unusual feeling of being part of a large family, since our own party of three- Mom, Grandma, and I- was my norm.

As I listened to the sermon, though, and joined in as best I could on unfamiliar songs, another thought came to mind.

This is your family, too.

Was this what it was like to hear from God? Those five words stayed with me throughout the service, a simple message, yet changing the way I looked at the people in this building. Not just Casey's family, but everyone here, at least those who trusted in Jesus, was connected. We did belong to the same family. *His* family.

Walking to our car after the service, I shared that thought with Mom.

"You're right," she agreed. "And I think just like any family, there are awkward moments." She grimaced, unlocking the car. "You want to know what *I* was thinking during the entire service? I was remembering that my daddy ran off with that woman, from my old church. I couldn't get that thought out of my mind this morning, Reese. No wonder Mother is reluctant to come back to church. She was betrayed, not just by her husband, but by another woman who was supposed to be following Jesus, too. By someone in her *church* family."

We got in the car and Mom cranked up the air conditioning since it was already a blazing hot day.

"Maybe..." I hesitated. This didn't sound like a churchy thing to say.

"Maybe what, hon? Spill it." Mom backed out of our parking space and started heading slowly to the parking lot exit, behind a bunch of other cars.

"Well, you know how in our business we have the Bless Their Heart couples? The ones who give us grief, and sometimes they're crazy rude? We put up with them because we get paid." Mom chuckled and I went on. "But maybe God has his own Bless Their Heart kids. The ones who screw up big time, and don't listen to him. They damage themselves and other people."

"Because they're still human, and we all mess up," Mom agreed, making a right turn on to the road.

"But God is still the same. He doesn't change, even if people do. Alrighty then, that's my first deep thought for the day, Mom." I adjusted the AC vent to direct more cool air towards me. "I do have another announcement at lunch, but you'll have to wait."

"Oh dear," Mom said with a groan. "I can't take any more big revelations, and after Ethan's surprise visit to our backyard the other night, I think your grandmother needs a break, too. Please, please let your announcement be an easy one."

"It's not," I promised, and smiled sweetly when Mom turned her head to glare at me.

Instead of our typical Sunday morning brunch, Mom and I were taking Grandma to lunch today at one of her favorite places, a tearoom in the historical district of our town. Grandma seemed delighted and had asked if she could invite another guest to join us. I expected it to be her friend Francine, so I was amazed when I saw a tall, handsome, blue-eyed young man striding across the crowded dining area towards our table. He looked all proper and dashing in his cobalt blue polo shirt and khakis.

He was also turning the heads of most ladies in the tearoom, both young and old, but this young man was looking at one person only, and it wasn't me. His smile zeroed in on Grandma, and she was grinning right back.

"You invited *Daniel*?" I raised my eyebrows.

"I heard that!" Daniel squeezed my shoulder as he slid into the empty chair between me and Grandma. "Why the shock? I can extend my pinkie over tea as well as anyone else."

"He's my friend, too," Grandma told me reprovingly, but there was a twinkle in her eye.

I eyed Daniel skeptically. I had seen this boy eat. "You do know that you'll leave here still hungry, right? Did you check the menu? It's all tiny sandwiches, quiche and scones, things like that."

"There's this new-fangled thing called 'fast food'," he retorted, making air quotation marks with his fingers. "I've heard it's the perfect follow-up to tearoom meals. Besides-"

Daniel turned to Grandma, again giving her his full attention. "I'm here for the delightful company anyway, ma'am, not just the food." Grandma nodded at him approvingly, and I rolled my eyes. Smooth, very smooth. That cocky Dixon charm at work!

When he turned his gaze to me, however, his smile wasn't quite the one he had given Grandma. This one was *mine*, the intimate smile I was learning that he reserved for only me. The one where his eyes lit up from a fire inside him that seemed to burn steadily, sending as clear a message as a look could give.

This guy liked me, He liked me an awful lot.

I decided to make my announcement more privately after all, inviting Daniel back to the house after lunch so he could hear it, too. We gathered once again at the kitchen table.

"I didn't want to risk anyone overhearing this at the tearoom, but I've decided I'm going to locate my father. I want to talk to him, and the sooner the better. If Ethan already knows who he is, then it's unlikely that he'll keep anything to himself, and Josh will find out about me one way or another. I just need to figure out the best way to go about this."

Nobody seemed surprised, and Mom was the first to speak. "That seems wise, Reese. Let's look at all the options."

"It's like a test I don't know how to study for," I admitted. "Is there one best way to do this? Should I call him first, or just show up at his house unannounced? Or try to set up a meeting?"

"We could all go with you to meet your dad, if you want," Daniel suggested. "To show solidarity, like 'Reese comes with a team. Meet Team Reese.'"

I smiled but shook my head. "That crossed my mind. Well, maybe not taking a whole team, but just you. I've been thinking, though. There's Josh, living his life all unknowing and going about his business. Then this perfect stranger comes knocking on his door, claiming to be his daughter. How will he react? How will *I* react to the way *he* reacts?"

Mom, Daniel, and I discussed the pros and cons of different scenarios, and then Grandma finally spoke up.

"Reese, in my opinion, you need to do what *you* are most comfortable with. I do suggest that if you decide to show up unannounced at his doorstep, you can't be sure how things will go, so having someone you trust close by is wise."

I guessed that Grandma was thinking about our backyard scene with Ethan, and I reached across the table to squeeze her hand. "Maybe I need to take you and your frying pan along, Grandma," I teased. "You make a good backup."

I looked over at Mom. "Ultimately, though, this is between me and Josh," I said gently, voicing the conviction that had been steadily growing in the back of my mind. "Not even you, Mom, just me and him. Father and daughter." Those last three words felt strange on my lips.

Mom nodded, looking wistful, and I wondered if she was remembering her own dad. Which was worse? Never having a father in your life, or having one who chose to break your mother's heart, ripping your family apart? Mom had her scars and I had mine, caused by people who loved us dearly but still made decisions that ultimately wounded us.

What about my own decisions? Would they help, or hurt other people?

"Let's pray about this," Grandma suggested unexpectedly, and she immediately lowered her head. Mom and I glanced at each other, surprised, then bowed our heads, too, along with Daniel. "Heavenly Father," Grandma began, and continued praying without any hesitation, her words simple, her voice strong.

"Amen!" Daniel seconded at the end of the prayer, and just like that, I knew what I was going to do.

CHAPTER 23

"I'll call Josh and set up a time to meet. If I just drive over to his house without warning, there's no guarantee that he'll be home, or there might be someone with him. Like a girlfriend, or fiancée. Who knows? He doesn't seem to be married.

"But once he actually sees me, I think he'll be convinced that I'm Ruby's daughter since we look so much alike. After all, your Uncle Danny figured out who I was within seconds of our meeting."

"True." Daniel offered me the last French fry, and I took it. Even I was a bit hungry after our tearoom meal, and we were now at his favorite burger place. He had ordered the house special, and we were sharing the fries.

Josh Lockwood only lived a couple of hours away, in a suburb of Dallas, so getting there wouldn't be a problem. Proving that I was Ruby's daughter shouldn't be a problem. Other than those two things, there were easily a hundred other things that *could* be a problem.

"He might insist on a paternity test. He might be furious with Mom, or even with me. He might think I'm just contacting him now to ask for money, or demand things. What if he does have a girlfriend who freaks out over this? Who knows? What prepares anyone for a situation like this?"

Daniel stretched his arms out across the back of the booth. "Well, let's see. Being kidnapped by aliens? Playing a life-or-death game where you don't know the rules? Jumping out of an airplane when you suspect your parachute might be just a backpack?" His tone was serious, but I saw the mischievous gleam in his eyes. "Want me to simulate some 'what would you do' situations, for practice?"

"No thanks, I'll just wing it. I'm beginning to think I'll spend most of my life just winging it."

"Well, we'll wing this one together," Daniel promised, sounding determined. "Whatever happens, we'll deal with it. Together." He reached across the table to offer me a fist bump, and I complied, deciding that another good kiss on the cheek would be a perfect follow-up, later.

Together had never sounded better.

We decided to spend the rest of this hot May afternoon in an air-conditioned theater, to see the latest action movie. As it turned out, many of our friends had the same idea and we were able to get seats together as a large group. Someone bought a jumbo tub of popcorn and started passing it down our row, offering it to anyone who wanted to take some.

"Seriously, Dixon? You've had two meals in the last three hours!" I shook my head, a smile tugging at my lips. "Where do you put it?"

"I'll sweat it off tomorrow with the rug rats," he said cheerfully, holding a handful of popcorn. "My basketball coach isn't nearly as tough on me as those kids are. Instead of 'summer camp' it should be called 'leave the counselors completely drained of any energy' camp."

I turned to respond, and as I did, I noticed a few other guys standing at the end of the row in front of us, looking for seats with the Rayburn crowd. They were on the football team, the same ones who had been at Ethan's house the night he posted about me. I froze, searching for Ethan.

Daniel followed my gaze. "He's not here."

"He might be." Ethan could still be in this theater, and I shivered a little. Was I afraid of him now? Had I arrived at the point where even thinking he was somewhere close by would make me nervous?

The lights dimmed and the previews started. Daniel put his arm around me protectively, and I scooted as close to him as I could get, with the arm rest still between us. For the next couple of hours, I did not need to be concerned. I was perfectly safe. It was just me and my superhero.

Including that way less cute one on the movie screen.

After Daniel took me home I went upstairs, practicing introductions in my head.

Hello, you don't know me, but I'm your daughter.

Hey, did you ever wonder whatever happened to your high school girlfriend who moved away her senior year?

Josh, my name is Reese Owens, and I'm seventeen years old. You are my father.

All of these seemed awkward and wrong, but I was resolute. I would pick one and just go with it, and it would happen now. I hadn't mentioned anything to Daniel since I literally made up my mind as I walked up the stairs. There didn't seem to be any reason to wait, however. The anxiety around this initial phone call would just weigh on my mind until I finally did the deed. Once it was done, who knew?

The outcome of this call was not entirely up to me. Much

depended on Josh Lockwood's response, and I would accept that, no matter what it was. There was no choice.

Shutting my bedroom door firmly behind me, I settled onto the middle of my bed, sitting cross-legged. I picked up my phone gingerly, like I had never used one before, and went to my contacts list. Josh's number was already entered.

Before I searched for his name, however, the phone started ringing and Ethan's number showed up on the screen. Distracted, I ended his call immediately and resumed my search for Josh's number.

Again, my phone started ringing and once more, it was Ethan. My nerves were already on edge, and this was not helping. Why hadn't I blocked his number before now? Irritated, I ended the call only to have it ring yet *again*, for the third time. Ethan seemed intent on reaching me, but I was equally determined now to block him, right this minute, with no delay. I managed to do that before there was a fourth call, and I sighed with both relief and frustration.

Relax. I rolled my shoulders and took a deep breath, saying a mental *"help me, Jesus!"* on the exhale. This time, my finger was hovering over the "call" icon when I heard the doorbell ring.

Not my problem. Mom or Grandma would answer the door.

I remembered then that Mom was having dinner with Daniel's uncle, an event she had seemed rather excited about, and Grandma was probably upstairs just like me, watching TV in her room as she usually did on most Sunday evenings. Hesitating, I considered Ethan's calls. What if that was him at the door, trying to get my attention since I wouldn't answer my phone? I needed to warn Grandma.

Exasperated, I got off the bed, opened my door and marched over to Grandma's room. Sure enough, she was reclined on her bed, snug and cozy, watching her detective show. The volume was loud, just how she liked it, and she probably hadn't heard the doorbell.

"Grandma, sorry to bother you but someone's at the front door and it could be Ethan."

She clicked off the TV immediately. "I'll call the police."

"Grandma..." I thought hard. "I don't *know* that it's Ethan and even if it is, it's not a crime to ring the doorbell. He's been calling and seems determined to reach me, so let's answer the door together and I'll hear him out one last time, and that's it. Grab the frying pan!"

My attempt at humor was met with a sour look as Grandma knelt and took a baseball bat out from under her bed. "Nice, Grandma. Do you always keep that under your bed?"

"I know how to use it! I played high school softball, you know." She started muttering about how she would have a security camera installed at our front door first thing tomorrow morning.

The doorbell rang again, and as we went down the stairs I texted Mom. She very likely would not be checking her phone during her meal, so I quickly forwarded the same message to Daniel.

> I'm home and we need Danny here right now!

Mom knew I would hate interrupting her date and would take my message seriously. It would freak her out, but an off-duty police officer might be an asset in this situation.

"Ethan's not dangerous," I reassured Grandma, one hand on the front doorknob as the doorbell rang again. She didn't look one bit convinced and held the bat up higher, ready to give anyone who threatened her granddaughter a solid whack. It wasn't that dark outside yet, but I turned the porch light on anyway, and opened the front door cautiously.

The stern look I had put on my face fell away. This person was definitely not Ethan. Ethan was not the one ringing our doorbell.

I had never met this man before, but I knew exactly who he was.

This was an older version of the teenage boy I had seen in Mom's high school yearbook. Here, standing on my front porch, was Josh Lockwood. My father.

My father had come to *me*.

Chapter 24

We stared at each other. I could not take my eyes off him, and it appeared to be mutual. Beside me, Grandma lowered her bat silently, waiting.

He finally broke the silence. "My name is Josh Lockwood." He nodded at Grandma apologetically. "You might remember me, ma'am. I dated your daughter many years ago? Anyway, I, um, I'm here for the meeting we set up." He looked at me, almost in awe. "I assume you are..." He couldn't seem to find words, and his expression was similar to what Uncle Danny's had been, as if he was speaking to a ghost.

"Reese," I told him softly, then repeated it more strongly. "Reese Owens." The first words I ever spoke to my father, and to my dismay I started tearing up.

Grandma took charge. "I do remember you, Josh. We're not aware of any meeting, but please come on in." He looked concerned but thanked her, and she led us both into the living room. "You sit here, and you sit there," pointing Josh to the sofa and me to an armchair. "Would you like a drink, Josh? Coffee or tea?"

When he declined, Grandma looked at him meaningfully.

"The two of you need to talk privately. But I'll just be right here in the kitchen, you understand?" Her tone was velvet, but her message was steel. *Don't hurt my granddaughter.*

Josh looked her in the eye, his expression almost appreciative. "Yes, ma'am." Grandma left and he looked back over at me, where I studied him, unsmiling.

Josh leaned forward as he sat on the sofa, both elbows on his knees, his hands clasped between them. A tall guy, his blond hair was trimmed short, and he still had the build of an athlete. In a detached way, I noted his Dallas Cowboys polo shirt, khaki shorts and spicy- smelling aftershave. Like Uncle Danny, he looked decent for a thirty-four-year-old. My gaze returned to his eyes, and I held them, the earlier tears gone.

"I thought you requested this meeting, Reese... wow, this is awkward. Do you even know why I'm here?" He sounded as nervous as I felt. It was time to just put everything out there.

"You're my father." My shoulders were rigid.

"Yes, I believe I am." With that he smiled for the first time, still seeming amazed along with another emotion I could not yet define. "I *hope* I am."

Something in my heart melted, and my shoulders relaxed.

I hope I am.

We started to talk, haltingly, two polite strangers trying to find their way to a possible friendship.

We barely made it past the basics before I heard a car screech to a stop in front of our house, and a door slam. "That will be Daniel," I guessed, and Josh raised his eyebrows. "He's my friend." He was more than just that, of course, but it was hardly a conversation for now.

Sure enough, I opened the front door to Daniel's worried expression. "Are you okay? Uncle Danny will be here as soon as he can. Whose car is that in your driveway?" He finally noticed Josh sitting on the couch and frowned. "Who are you?"

Josh stood up, but before he could say anything Grandma appeared from the kitchen. "Daniel, I can explain. Everything's all right. Would you please come join me on the patio? I have iced tea."

Daniel hesitated, then responded to Grandma's request, reluctantly. "Yes, ma'am." Clearly he didn't want to leave me alone with this man, and Josh recognized this fact because he stepped forward, holding out his hand.

"I'm Josh Lockwood." We both watched Daniel's scowl change to recognition, then surprise. He extended his own hand and shook Josh's firmly.

"Daniel Dixon." He turned to me. "I'll be right out there if you need me."

His concern warmed my heart. "I know." I leaned in closer then, giving him a quick hug, and the look in his eyes as I pulled away about curled my toes.

Josh watched all of this with frank interest. "So, he's just a friend?" he asked, as Daniel joined Grandma outside, and we both settled back into our seats. Wait, was he fishing for information? Wasn't it a little early on for that?

Josh noticed my hesitation because he hastily backtracked. "That is none of my business, Reese, I'm sorry."

"No, it's okay," I told him, and it was. "Daniel and I, well, we're keeping things simple." I left it at that, and Josh dipped his chin in acknowledgment.

"That's a good decision. Keeping things simple, I like that. It's totally appropriate for your age. Your mother and I did not keep things simple, and here we are, years later. But look at you, Reese."

This time it was his eyes that were shining with tears unshed. "You are a gift from God. I know we just met, and there's so much ground to cover, and we have a long way to go, but... I'm hoping, with your permission, that we can get to know each other better. Figure some things out.

I nodded, cautiously. "It will take time."

"The best things always do," he replied. There was sadness in his voice.

"So, about this meeting you said I had requested? Why did you- "

Before I could finish my question, I heard two more car doors slam outside. "I forgot to let Mom know everything's okay," I moaned. "I guess Grandma forgot, too."

Josh looked nervous again. "Is that your- "

The front door flung open, and Uncle Danny stepped inside, grim-faced and alert. Mom was right behind him, and she looked like she was ready to wrestle a grizzly bear.

"*Josh*?" Her voice was shocked.

"Yes, Ruby, it's me. Hey, aren't you Danny?" Josh seemed surprised, too. "Danny Dixon?"

"In the flesh," Danny drawled. "Long time no see. What's going on, Reese?"

Grandma and Daniel came in from the backyard at that point, and for a few minutes it was orderly chaos as explanations were made and anxieties simmered down. By the time Josh and I were alone again in the living room, though, I had only one more question for him, the one I had started to ask him earlier. After that we didn't linger, both of us agreeing that we would meet up again soon- very soon- for a longer conversation. The hardest part was over, Josh declared. We had met for the first time, and we both wanted to get to know each other better.

This was progress. A first huge, major step.

I felt like a deflated balloon, though, as I got ready for bed later. This meeting with my father hadn't gone at all the way I had hoped for, amid all the interruptions and lack of privacy most of the time, with even a baseball bat thrown in the mix. Brushing out my hair, I heard my phone ding with an incoming message.

> Team Reese showed up after all. Are you disappointed?

Could that boy read my mind? I considered Daniel's question. Team Reese *had* shown up. They were there for me. I had prayed such a tiny prayer for help earlier this evening, and God had answered in such a big, unexpected way.

And amid the chaos, Josh told me I was a gift.

Not a burden, or an unwelcome intrusion into his life, but a gift!

Thank you.

I texted Daniel back.

> I was, but now I'm mostly grateful. I could not love Team Reese any more than I do tonight!

His response was immediate.

> I'll always have your back, Reese. Sweet dreams.

Sleep did not come easily, this Sunday night. I stared at the ceiling, reviewing the meeting with my father and the words we exchanged, over and over.

But when I woke up the next morning, after finally falling into a fitful sleep, there was a smile on my face.

CHAPTER 25

"Are you ready?"

I gave a thumbs up, determined. "Let's get this over with."

Mom rang the doorbell, and Ethan's mother answered immediately. "Please come in," she said politely, her smile brittle. "Have a seat."

Mr. and Mrs. Hall were reluctant to meet with us at all but had finally agreed when the talk of protective orders and potential background checks came up, as well as the fact that Ethan would soon turn eighteen and no longer be a minor. They insisted on hosting this meeting in their own home, however, and I soon understood why.

Besides Ethan and his parents, another man was seated in their living room. Standing immediately and extending his hand, he introduced himself as Alex Garcia, a friend of the family who happened to be an attorney. Mom and I hadn't been informed that he would be here, but it didn't bother me.

Just tell your story. Stick to the facts. Uncle Danny's advice echoed in my mind, and as Mom and I sat down, side by side on the luxurious leather couch, I gave her arm a little squeeze. She looked my way and winked. Ruby backed down for no one when it came to her daughter, and this time she had talked things over with Jesus. In other words, she felt unstoppable.

I glanced at Ethan, who was sitting in a chair that had probably been brought in from the kitchen. He was looking down, jiggling one of his legs nervously. Mr. Hall also looked uncomfortable.

The lawyer spoke first. "We are gathered here today"- I almost giggled. Was this a funeral? Forcing myself to stay composed, I kept listening.

"-we'll hear both sides of the situation and hopefully resolve all misunderstandings. Miss Owens, would you care to begin?"

"Yes, sir." I started at the beginning as Danny had instructed. Ethan and I had been friends, and nothing more. We hung out and went to a couple of school events together. When it became clear that he wanted more than just a friendship, I declined. He seemed upset with me.

"All of this is normal high school stuff," Mr. Hall interrupted, throwing up his hands in the air.

"Please go on," Mr. Garcia told me, ignoring the outburst.

I told about the social media post, the punches thrown between Ethan and Daniel, the meeting with my school counselor, and how Ethan tried to keep contacting me. He came into our backyard uninvited and texted me to meet him there, and I told them how uneasy this made me feel, to the point where I called the police. At this point Ethan interrupted.

"Her grandmother threatened *me*! I was the one who was uneasy!"

"Shut up, Ethan," his father growled, and the lawyer encouraged me to continue.

"The first time he sneaked into our backyard, he eavesdropped on a private conversation I was having about my biological father, who I had never met. I mentioned his name, and Ethan took it upon himself to not only look up my father's location, but to also contact him through a phone call. He told Josh- my father- that I was too nervous to contact him myself and that I had asked him to do it for me. He told Josh all about me and sent him my picture."

I took a breath, steadying my voice. "My father showed up last Sunday evening at my door. I didn't know he was coming, but Ethan did. Josh had asked Ethan to set up a meeting between the two of us, because he was led to believe that Ethan was speaking on my behalf. Ethan gave Josh my address and a time, and pretended to Josh that I knew all about it. I don't know why Ethan kept this a secret from me, but at the last minute I'm guessing he had second thoughts, and he tried to call and warn me. To let me know my father was coming to meet me for the very first time."

I stared at Ethan directly, and he finally met my eyes. "You lied to Josh, and you took something valuable from me. You stole my right to speak for myself, to decide how I wanted to introduce myself to a father I had never met before."

"None of this constitutes bullying, besides that first social media incident," Mr. Hall interrupted again. "Ethan's choices may have been poor, but he never threatened this young lady. He did her no physical harm. In fact, he even tried to help her in his own way."

Mom tensed up beside me and I could tell she was about ready to throw out some of her own "opinions." Mr. Garcia simply held up his hand, however, and matter-of-factly told Ethan to give his own account.

Ethan gave a rambling defense, full of his disappointment in our friendship, how I wouldn't let him be a part of my life even though our relationship had been great, and how he was always acting in my best interests. It was a whiny, self-centered, and disturbing speech, and I noticed Mr. Hall shift in his chair. His mom sat perfectly still, her face ashen. I felt sorry for both of them.

In the end, Mr. Garcia thanked Mom and I for initiating the meeting. "I'm speaking as a friend of the family here, and not as their attorney, but hopefully this situation will be resolved satisfactorily, in the best interests of everyone." He hesitated and spoke to the group at large. "Counseling might be a good idea."

"I agree," Mr. Hall said immediately. "It could help this young lady deal with some of her, shall we say, father issues."

"I believe Mr. Garcia was also talking about your son," Mom said coolly, and Ethan's dad looked at his friend, eyebrows raised.

"That is correct," he confirmed, and didn't flinch when Mr. Hall looked as if he could spit nails. "We'll talk some things over later, David. I'll see myself out."

Mom and I followed him to the front door, more than ready to leave this house, but paused when Mrs. Hall called my name.

"Reese?" I looked back at her and tried to smile. I had always liked Ethan's mom, the couple of other times I had met her. She still looked pale and drawn.

"Yes, ma'am?"

Drawing closer to Mom and me, her look was beseeching. "I'm truly sorry about all of this. It won't happen again. This-this behavior will stop."

I didn't see how she could possibly guarantee that, but I appreciated her words. "I hope so. It *must* stop." I felt sorry for her obvious pain. "I'll pray for your family."

I had never promised that to anyone before, but I meant it. Even a simple prayer could be powerful, and Ethan needed help. Their whole family did.

Nothing was completely resolved as we left Ethan's house

and drove home. I supposed that was just life. Ethan's story, as well as my own, was on the "to be continued" shelf, just like the story of me and Josh.

The story of me and my father, fortunately, seemed to be headed in a positive direction. Over the next few weeks, Josh made the drive to visit with me when he could, and we also scheduled video calls every few days. Some lasted only five minutes and others up to an hour! Mom even joined in a couple of times, and we were gradually becoming more comfortable with each other.

As for Mom and Uncle Danny's renewed friendship? That was starting to look promising, too.

CHAPTER 26

This story, however, Daniel's and mine? Never dull. Guess who else was turning eighteen?

"Truth or dare," Daniel said one Sunday evening, as we sat in my backyard eating nachos. We were talking and watching the fireflies start to appear in the woods just behind our back fence.

We still played this game every now and then, some questions thoughtful and deep, others lighthearted. Daniel always took a dare, and I always chose the truth option. Tonight, however, I decided to shake things up.

"Dare!"

"Whoa, a change of pattern," Daniel said, his eyebrows raised. "I'd better make this dare a good one then, in case you never choose it again. On the other hand, I can't go overboard, or I'll scare you off from the option forever. Tricky."

"Overthink much? Just pick something! Remember I have the right to pass, of course."

"Of course." He studied me. "Okay, I've got one. I dare you to ride a rollercoaster with me."

I tilted my head, considering. Rollercoasters were not my

favorite, but I could usually handle them. "All right, I can do that, but I sense a problem."

"A problem already anticipated," he replied smugly, leaning back in his chair with a grin. "We'll travel to a place that actually has a roller coaster. We can do it on my birthday in two weeks!"

"Not one that goes upside down," I told him, already regretting my quick agreement. "Or backwards."

"Deal and deal. Nope," he said, holding up a hand when I opened my mouth to add to my restrictions list. *"No más.* We'll pick the coaster when we get there."

"There" turned out to be a large amusement park in the Dallas area, and plans were made. Daniel took the day off, and Grandma agreed to let me have both Friday and Saturday off. Together we made the two-hour drive to the park on the Friday morning of his birthday. At my father's invitation, we would spend Friday night at his condo, have lunch together on Saturday, and afterwards Ethan and I would drive back home.

The day was breezy and cloudy, a welcome combination for a July day in Texas, and the park was packed. Neither of us had been here in years, so we had fun revisiting all our favorite rides.

"I'm soaked!" I shrieked at the bottom of the log flume ride, laughing. "Let's go again!"

"Nope, young lady, three times is enough with these lines," Daniel told me, leaning over my shoulder from where he sat right behind me on the ride. "Besides, it's *coaster* time! You've delayed long enough."

"I have not!" We stepped out of our log carefully as the ride attendant stood by to assist and headed for the exit. "Besides, you were the one screaming like a girl on that log ride! Can *you* handle a roller coaster?"

"You might have to hold my hand," he said innocently, and I immediately took his in mine.

"Lead on, Dixon. I've got this."

We had already decided on a coaster that met both of our specs, and Josh led the way to that area of the park. After a relatively short wait, we made it to the front of the line, where to my shock we were told that we could sit in the very first car. At the *front* of the first car. I gulped.

"We don't have to," Daniel told me quickly. "We can switch with someone else. Or we can let others go ahead of us while we wait for the next set of cars." The attendant prompted us to decide, while the previous riders started unloading. I was about to decline when I looked at Daniel's face.

He was so excited, so *gleeful*. He loved coasters! This was his thing, and he had asked me along for the ride. Or dared me, to be exact.

"Happy birthday," I told him, resigning myself to terror. "First car it is."

His face lit up even more. "You won't regret it," he reassured me. "I'll scream extra loud just for you."

We loaded up and the attendant checked our harnesses, making sure all the riders were secure. "Enjoy the ride!" she called out, waving to everyone as our coaster started moving forward.

The first few climbs and dips were mild, and it was fun being up so high, the wind in our faces. "You're doing great, legend," Daniel called out, and then we started climbing a higher slope, and I tensed. This first big drop wasn't too bad, however, and I didn't scream even once. I even giggled at the bottom, but could hardly catch my breath before the next, steeper climb began. We inched up, and up, slowly, and my stomach started to clench.

"How tall is this thing? This is insane!"

"You'll be fine! Ask me truth or dare, Reese! Quick!"

"What?" I could barely think.

"Fast! Ask me!"

We were almost at the top. "All right, truth or dare?"

"I choose truth, both the question and the answer! It's a combo this time!"

Truth? Daniel never chose truth, and what was this about a combo? As we reached the top, though, he continued hurriedly. "Just listen, okay?"

Our view at the top, for just a second, was stunning. The entire park lay below us, colorful, full of rides and happy people. I gripped my handrail tighter, ready to squeeze my eyes shut.

Then, in the split second before our car started to drop, Daniel yelled at the top of his voice.

"I LOVE YOU, REESE OWENS!"

And then we dropped.

I barely noticed the whooshing, crazy fast descent. The g-forces didn't faze me. I was oblivious, my thoughts as light as a feather carried gently on a breeze, finally coming to rest on a patch of soft, green grass, just as our coaster slowed down, ready to pull into the ride station where we would unload.

As we slowed, I looked over at Daniel, dazed, and he met my gaze, grinning. This guy chose me. He said he loved me. Even more astonishing, I believed him.

We climbed out of the coaster and headed to the ride exit with the rest of the laughing, excited riders. Grabbing his hand, I dragged Daniel to the first empty bench I could find.

He put his arm around me, tucking me in close as we sat for a few minutes, quietly watching people walk by. My heart was beating fast, yet my mind was clear and calm. I had said these words to a boy before, and I meant them, but at the time I didn't understand what it meant to truly love someone.

I did now.

"Daniel? That was *epic*."

He looked down at me, his blue eyes sparkling. Daniel was so full of joy and didn't seem to expect me to react to his declaration in any certain way. There was no pressure. *Love protects, trusts, hopes, perseveres. I love you, Reese Owens.*

I put my hand around the back of Daniel's neck and pulled his face closer to mine. "By the way, Dixon, I love you too, and that's the truth. The genuine, absolute, certified... truth." My last word was a whisper.

The simple, sweet kiss that followed was not about old dreams. It had nothing to do with former, sincere, heartfelt wishes and hopes. Instead, it was all about true, and altogether daring, choices.

Choices that would build the foundation for brand new dreams.

Dear Reader,

Thanks for reading Reese and Daniel's story! Like theirs, your own story is still in progress.

As a bonus, check out a couple of songs from Reese's playlist:

"All This Time," Britt Nicole

"Truth Be Told," Matthew West and Carly Pearce

Also, please take the time to leave a review on Amazon and/or Goodreads. Every single one is appreciated more than you know!

Ready to read Casey's story? Check out "Feelin' The Chemistry", Book One in the High School 101 Series, here!

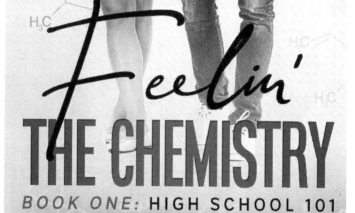

Feelin'
THE CHEMISTRY

BOOK ONE: HIGH SCHOOL 101

MELISSA KNIGHT

Made in the USA
Columbia, SC
19 August 2024